A Mystery of Murder

A Jan Christopher Mystery

Helen Hollick

Taw River Press

A Mystery Of Murder
A Jan Christopher Mystery - Episode 2
By Helen Hollick

ISBN-13:
978-1-8381318-2-1 Paperback
978-1-8381318-3-8 e-book

Published by Taw River Press
https://www.tawriverpress.co.uk

READERS' COMMENTS for
A MIRROR MURDER (episode 1)

"I sank into this gentle cosy mystery story with the same enthusiasm and relish as I approach a hot bubble bath, (in fact this would be a great book to relax in the bath with!) and really enjoyed getting to know the central character, a shy young librarian, and the young police officer who becomes her romantic interest. The nostalgic setting of the 1970s was balm, so clearly evoked, and although there is a murder at the heart of the story, it was an enjoyable comfort read." *Debbie Young, author of the Sophie Sayers cosy mysteries*

"A delightful read about a murder in North-East London. Told from the viewpoint of a young library assistant, the author draws on her own experience to weave an intriguing tale." *Richard Ashen – South Chingford Community Library*

"Well-paced with action interspersed with red herrings, shady suspects, and some nice passages of information which, ultimately are inconsequential, but are actually very interesting. Characterisations are excellent – especially Aunt Madge! I love Aunt Madge!"

"An enjoyable read with a twist in who done it. I spent the entire read trying to decide what was a clue and what wasn't... Kept me thinking. I call that a success."

"A delicious distraction... What a lovely way to spend an afternoon!"

"I really identified with Jan – the love of stories from an early age, and the careers advice – the same reaction I got – no one thought being a writer was something a working class girl did! The character descriptions are wonderfully done."

"Brilliant! I'm so enjoying Helen's well-researched murder mystery. I'm not giving anything away here, except to say there's lots of nostalgia, and detail that readers of a certain age (me included) will lap up. A jolly good read. In my opinion, it would make a great television series."

To all the people who once lived in my Devon farmhouse
– the spirits of the past.

Thank you for your very pleasant company.

1

WHEN DOUBTS ARISE?

The thought of driving all the way from London to Devon with my boyfriend, Laurie, for Christmas was exciting, but tinged with a smattering of reluctance. It would mean leaving my Uncle Toby and Aunt Madge, behind. I'd not had a Christmas or a New Year without them since they'd adopted me when I was orphaned at five years old. At almost nineteen, independence was knocking at the door, but all the same, I was concerned about leaving them for the duration of the festivities. Concerns which Aunt Madge soon put an end to.

"Goodness, Jan, we've been looking forward to a Christmas on our own for the past, I don't know how many years!"

I wasn't sure if she was being serious or joking.

They had taken me under their wing after Uncle Toby's brother – my father, a Detective Inspector – had been shot dead, and my mother... well, she died soon after, but we never talked about that. All I know, she had been under severe mental strain from when my identical twin, June, died after an illness. I still resented June because she was the second born, and got the name 'June' for the month we were conceived. I got the name of the month we were prematurely born – January. Fortunately, everyone calls me Jan.

Uncle Toby's response to my worries about Christmas was less blunt. "Laurie is already taking leave, so we can't all be off on merry jaunts at the same time, Jan. The crime rate would soar, and Chingford Police wouldn't cope."

My uncle, in his working capacity, was Detective Chief Inspector Tobias Christopher. Laurie – Lawrence Walker – had recently been promoted to be his Detective Sergeant bagman. Two important people within the realm of law enforcement, although, I suspected that the North London suburban town of Chingford would survive without them both for a few days. There were, after all, *other* men (and a few women) in CID. Although, maybe these others were not as competent – but then, my opinion is severely biased.

For myself, I was quite happy to take several days off from working as an assistant in our local library. It was always busy in the run-up to Christmas closing, and while I would miss out on the boxes of chocolates and tins of buttery shortbread given to the staff by appreciative members of the public, my already too broad waistline would not suffer from it.

My main fear, however, was meeting Laurie's parents. I had spoken to them on the telephone several times and they seemed nice, but I had been going out with Laurie since late July – would they assume that our relationship was becoming serious?

Come to that, did *I* assume it was serious? By accepting the invitation, was I committing myself to a possible life as a policeman's wife? Or was I reading too much into things? I mean, spending Christmas with your boyfriend's family didn't mean a marriage proposal, did it? Or did it? Then there was the question, did I, or didn't I, *want* it to mean just that?

Had I known what was to happen soon after we arrived at Mr and Mrs Walker's lovely old West Country house though, my apprehension would have dwindled to nothing.

A grisly murder was discovered, which somewhat tarnished the traditional jolly Christmas Spirit...

2

ARRIVAL

"Hello! Did you have a good journey?" Mr Walker, average height and weight and with slightly salt-and-peppered hair, held out his hand to shake mine, then changed his mind and drew me into a welcoming bear hug. He smelled of pipe tobacco and wet dog, two friendly, homely, aromas.

"Hello, Miss Christopher, Happy Christmas. I'm so glad you could come." Mrs Walker was more reserved and formal. A little shorter than myself, slightly dumpier. She held out her hand for me to shake before turning to her son.

"Lawrence, pet, you've put on weight. What have they been feeding you up in London? Fish and chips with more chips than fish, I suspect." She leaned forward for Laurie to kiss her carefully powdered cheek. Her short hair had been professionally styled and coloured to an attractive auburn. Her pink lipstick was recently re-applied – smartly dressed as if she were about to go to an important Women's Institute meeting or something, not spending an afternoon at home with her family.

It sounded strange hearing someone call him

'Lawrence'. No one else did. Uncle Toby called him 'Walker', surnames only where professionalism was concerned. 'Old School' habits and all that. To me, he was just Laurie.

"Hello, Mum, Dad. You'd better go and let that dog out before she breaks the door down," Laurie said with a laugh as he opened the car boot and reached in to retrieve our cases. He ignored the two cardboard boxes which were hidden under a blanket; they had gayly wrapped Christmas presents secreted inside them. I'd been forbidden to poke around inside Laurie's box, which was fair enough as I had forbidden him to peer into mine.

I was stiff. I stretched my shoulders and arched my back; it had been a long drive down from London, despite the newly opened (that very day!) section of the M5 motorway between Maidenhead and Swindon. It had been rather exciting to be one of the first to drive along it!

"Let me take that!" Mr Walker took hold of my case and mock-grimaced as he pretended to stagger under its supposed heavy weight. I didn't have much inside it: all the usual necessities and my favourite teddy. (His name is Bee Bear, on account of him wearing a black and yellow striped jumper when I was given him as a present for my sixth birthday. The jumper is long gone, and yes, he is a little worn and moth-eaten. But I love him.)

My wellingtons, heavy-duty mac and comfortable walking shoes were also in the car boot: we were in the country, and the countryside meant suitable outdoor apparel, but I didn't need them yet, so I left them beside the Christmas boxes.

"Goodness, it's cold out here! There will be a frost tonight, maybe snow coming soon. Did you close the greenhouse door, Alfred?" Mrs Walker said as she peered up the path, which ran alongside a thick hedgerow of copper beech, holly, hawthorn, honeysuckle and wild dog rose. None of it was flowering this time of year, but there were a few patches of glossy, red holly berries that hadn't been devoured by the birds yet. I was a townie, but Aunt Madge knew about trees and flowers and had taught me many of their names ever since I was a little girl. I looked along the path to where I could see the glass roof of a large greenhouse, and what appeared to be a well-tended vegetable plot. Aunt Madge would be in her element – she loved gardening.

Mrs Walker was right, the air was cold and crisp, our breath floated in plumes of mist and there was already a light sparkle of frost appearing on the windscreen of the Walker's car, parked in the lane beside the hedge. I noticed an open-fronted barn a little further along the lane and wondered why the car was out here, not in there.

"Yes, light of my life, woman of the house, I did close up the greenhouse. Our winter veg and salads are all tucked up, with the paraffin heater lit to keep their rooty-tooty toes warm. And snow would be ideal." Mr Walker was grinning, "Use a broom to sweep it off and it cleans the glass admirably. Put your car down in the barn later, Laurie. We'll use mine tonight. Let's get inside for now; as much as I welcome the cleaning potential of snow, we don't want to stand out here any longer than we have to!"

Tonight? I wondered. What was a car needed for?

Mr Walker offered me his arm and, smiling as broad as the full moon which was just rising behind the trees and glowing bright against the twilight-blue sky, led me towards the house, in the opposite direction of the greenhouse, down the path which ran alongside the hedge.

"Yes, do go on in – take that case from your father, Lawrence. Alfred, you know you are not supposed to carry heavy things after *your operation*." Mrs Walker part-whispered, part-mouthed the last two words.

I glanced over my shoulder at Laurie who was behind me. *What operation?*

He laughed. "Hernia, more than eight months ago, so well past the sell-by date."

I frowned at him, not understanding.

He laughed. "It's a family joke. In my college days, I worked Saturdays in Marks and Spencer's store room; they label their perishable food with a 'sell by' date. I now use the phrase for anything that is out of date. Recovery from operations included."

I smiled back at him, teased, "So your battered old car is well past its sell-by date?"

He snorted. "No way, she'll go a good few thousand miles yet!"

Mr Walker, quite easily carrying my case, his other arm still linked through mine, winked at me. "Only because the rust holds it together."

Beside the house, the path broadened out into a square of paving stones which had two steps leading up into the shelter of a slate-roofed porch and the front door, behind which a dog was barking furiously. Mrs Walker brushed past us and, turning the brass knob, opened the door. A black Labrador came bouncing out, tail twirling like a whirligig. Laurie had already told me about Bess, I think he missed her now that he lived in North London. She didn't know which one of us to lick to death first, then realised Laurie was there and her excitement turned to ecstasy.

"Hello, Bess, old girl!" he laughed as he fended off her doggy hugs and kisses. "Goodness, what a welcome!"

"Push her down, Lawrence, you know she gets too boisterous. Bess! Go in! On your bed!"

I rather thought Mrs Walker's orders futile as Bess, ignoring her, her brown eyes adoring, had no intention of moving away from Laurie.

An evergreen honeysuckle sprawled up the wall and tumbled over the porch roof, I'd already noticed the chatter of birds, and as we'd approached, the sound had grown louder with dozens of agitated little birds flitting about within the tangle of leaves and branches.

"Sparrows," Mr Walker explained when he noticed my expression. "The honeysuckle houses dozens of them, and they squabble with each other of an evening for the best roosting spots – it's the equivalent of a TV soap. *Coronation Street* a la sparrow style."

I laughed. "Which one is Ena Sharples or Elsie Tanner?"

The house – a typical Devonshire building, part stone, part white-limed cobb – was situated one mile from the village of Chappletawton. It was an old house, built, so Laurie had told me, in the early 1600s. There were bullet holes in one wall, apparently, where during the English Civil War a troop of Fairfax's billeted Roundheads, prior to the battle of Torrington, had decided to do some target practice. Valley View Farm, as the house was called, for obvious reasons, was no longer a farm but still boasted its name and an E-shaped two-acres of land orientated north-west to south-east. The house itself formed the middle prong of the E, with the greenhouse and vegetable patch the downhill boundary 'prong', and, as I was to discover later, a well-kept garden ascending to an orchard and woodland area made the other prong. Beyond the boundary hedges, a spectacular view across this part of the Taw Valley.

The rest of what had once been a dairy farm, had

been absorbed into the down-the-hill neighbour's property, Lower Valley View Farm. I had the feeling that Devonians of the past were not very imaginative where naming places was concerned, especially when the somewhat dilapidated smallholding at the up-the-hill end of the long, narrow, high-hedge and bank access lane, was called Higher Valley View Farm. I'll leave you to guess what the lane itself was called. (Correct. Valley View Lane.)

With Bess leading the way, tail still wagging as if there were no tomorrow, we went indoors into a square, slate-tiled hallway with doors leading off it to left and right. Straight ahead, a reverse-L-shaped, wide oak staircase, while against the wall beside the front door, which Mrs Walker hastily closed behind us, was a beautiful old longcase grandfather clock. As we entered, it melodically chimed the hour of four. I discreetly checked my watch. The clock was ten minutes fast. Mr Walker took my coat and added it to others on a line of wooden coat hooks. Laurie put our suitcases at the bottom of the stairs, ready to take up, and escorted me to the left, into a comfortably furnished, large sitting room.

It was like stepping back into the seventeenth century! Originally, so Laurie told me, this had been the kitchen and family living space: there were low beams and the most enormous fireplace. A huge Yule Log, a complete length of tree trunk, filled its width. With smaller logs stacked around it the impression was more like a garden bonfire!

Dominating the room was a bauble, tinsel and paper-chain-bedecked Christmas tree. The rest of the room was festooned with more paper chains and sparkly Christmas decorations draped between the beams, with coloured candles in pretty holders surrounded by bunches of holly and ivy spread along

9

the mantlepiece and windowsills. The effect was stunning.

"Oh, what a beautiful room!" I exclaimed, standing stock-still just inside the door.

"Why, thank you, pet," Mrs Walker answered with a pleased smile. "We wanted to make a festive effort for you and Lawrence."

"We?" Mr Walker said with a loud guffaw, "I'm the one who had to creak up and down the ladders, dodging the cobwebs, to put everything up. I hope you don't mind spiders, Miss Christopher? The little buggers get everywhere in these old houses!"

"Not quite so little sometimes!" Laurie chuckled, spreading his hands wide to indicate an arachnid as big as a dinner plate.

I did mind, but kept quiet. I can tolerate spiders as long as they stay where they are meant to be – well out of my way.

Mrs Walker tutted. "Don't exaggerate, Lawrence, and mind your language, Alfred. Oh, on your bed, you silly dog. I do apologise, Miss Christopher, she gets over-excited when we have company. We're a bit out of the way down here. We don't get many visitors."

I didn't mind the dog, but hoped Mrs Walker wasn't going to keep calling me 'Miss Christopher' for the entire holiday.

"Please, do call me Jan," I begged.

"Go on in," Laurie said, nudging me forward, his hand gentle on my elbow. "Ma, I hope you've got the kettle on?"

"Of course I have. Tea, Miss Chris... *Jan*, pet?"

The last was directed at me, but she was gone, trotting off across the hallway towards, I assumed, the kitchen. *Pet*? I knew it was a northern term of endearment, but Mrs Walker didn't sound as if she came from the

Newcastle area. Laurie had told me that his parents had moved to Devon from Buckinghamshire when he was seven, so I was a little mystified by the Geordie term.

"Come and sit down," Mr Walker said to me. "Take this chair near the fire to warm yourself up."

I noticed a book on a small coffee table next to the chair, atop it, a pair of spectacles. "I'm not taking your seat, am I, Mr Walker?" I looked at the book title – the habit of a bookworm and a library assistant. "A.L. Frederick? Oh, I love his thrillers!" I said. "His idea of a spy masquerading as a hotel inspector is genius, the character can go anywhere in the world. This one is set in India, isn't it?"

Mr Walker beamed with pleasure. "No, no, sit there, my dear, and yes, India; it's his latest release – and it's Alf."

Laurie grinned as he sat down on one of the two settees, prodding at a pile of cushions as he did so, while simultaneously fending off Bess who was trying to climb into his lap. "I warn you, Jan, Mum will be in with the baster soon – anyone who sits too long in that chair gets roasted because the fire's so hot. That's why there are so many seats in here – we change places every half-hour like a parody of the Mad Hatter's Tea Party to cool down a bit."

Mrs Walker came back in carrying a tray with cups, saucers, sugar bowl, milk jug and a plate of chocolate biscuits. Laurie jumped up to take it from her, set it down on the coffee table and wandered over to a piano in the corner of the room.

"Tea's brewing," Mrs Walker announced, "but not too many of these biscuits, we'll be eating dinner prompt at six as there's the Bonfire Carol Service at seven. I hope shepherd's pie is all right for you, Jan pet? And don't get engrossed in that piano, Lawrence, you'll have plenty of time to tinkle over these next few days."

Laurie ignored her and opened the lid, ran his fingers across the keys. He was a proficient player. I could see that he was itching to 'tinkle' as Mrs Walker had termed it. I hid a smile. Aunt Madge used the same term to visit the 'little room'.

I answered his mum about the shepherd's pie with a friendly smile, for it dawned on me that perhaps she was just as nervous at meeting me as I was at meeting her? It was one of my favourites; minced lamb with a topping of creamy mashed potato. 'Cottage pie' was the same, but made with beef instead of lamb.

"Oh, yes, thank you..." but she had already gone, trotting back towards the kitchen. (Yes, I know, but she really *did* trot!)

"When's Gran coming?" Laurie asked. He'd left the piano to return to the biscuits and was now speaking through a mouthful of crumbs. "I half expected her to be here already."

"Picking her and her broomstick up from the station at eleven-fifteen tomorrow morning," his dad said. "So we've one evening of respite before we need to hang up the garlic."

"Garlic is to ward off vampires, not witches," Laurie corrected.

"My mother-in-law is both," Mr Walker said, then hastily coughed as his wife returned.

"What's that?" Mrs Walker was carrying an enormous blue floral, bone-china teapot. (Walking this time; I guess it isn't easy trotting while carrying a full teapot.)

"Strong brewer's tea or weak dairymaid, Jan pet? Sugar?"

Again, I had no chance to answer. Fortunately, I got medium-weak 'dairymaid' with one sugar, which is how I like my tea. She handed cups all round, then sat down, chatting about nothing in particular, although no one else got much of a chance to say anything.

Bess had abandoned her enthusiastic welcoming and was stretched out on the rug in front of the fire, her ears and legs twitching every so often dreaming of chasing rabbits. I'd never had a dog, although I'd often asked for one throughout my childhood, but Aunt Madge preferred cats – and horses.

Mr Walker – Alf – put more logs on the fire, tucking them round and over the Yule Log, which he'd told me would burn slowly right through until twelfth night. The air was filled with the sweet scent of applewood as the new logs caught, then Mrs W started clearing away the tea cups, although I would have loved a refill.

"Don't forget to take those suitcases upstairs, Lawrence. Your own room, of course, and I've put your young lady in the Rose Room."

I had a vision of something out of Snow White or Sleeping Beauty, and wondered how far the Rose Room was from Laurie's. We had slept together, taking all the proper precautions, but Laurie had already warned me that, "Ma won't approve of 'relations'."

When we went upstairs, after I had made a quick telephone call home to say we'd arrived safe and in one piece, my suspicion was confirmed; Laurie's bedroom was at one end of a long landing, while mine was at the *other* end and up another flight of narrow stairs. Stairs which creaked as much as the uncarpeted, but sheepskin rugged, wooden floor of the landing. No chance of sneaking into each other's rooms in the middle of the night up here! There was one bathroom, white, not the sickly green avocado colour that was fashionable for many UK households, near the bottom of 'my' stairs, and a separate toilet next to it. There was also a 'lavvy', as Mrs Walker had called it, downstairs adjoining a scullery and back entrance porch, "Where we keep our boots and old coats." Indoors, thank goodness, not an outdoor privy full of spiders and icicles with squares of cut up newspaper for toilet paper, or the scratchy, hard Izal stuff that doubled nicely as tracing paper!

It was a comfortable bedroom: little pink roses on the wallpaper, bedspread and eiderdown on the single bed; a bowl of sweet-smelling potpourri on the dressing table. A pink handbasin in one corner framed by a built-in cupboard – which was a relief as it meant I didn't have to share the bathroom to wash. There was also a central heating radiator, which, when I put my hand on it, was nice and warm. I really don't know why I was expecting a cranky old two-bar electric fire that gave off more smoking dust than actual heat – or even worse, no heating at all! There was no reason to assume that Devonshire houses were still in the Dark Ages, this *was* 1971 after all!

Left alone to unpack, I transferred my few belongings from my case into the wardrobe and chest-of-drawers, shaking the creases out of the couple of decent frocks, then laid out my hairbrush, face cream and make-up on the dressing table, tucked my nightdress under the pillows, and sat Bee Bear on top, from where he proffered his usual congenial smile back at me. I went to hang my dressing gown behind the door and felt it being pushed open. Emitting a squeak of surprise, I scooted backwards. Laurie's head, bearing a huge grin, appeared.

"You OK?"

"You made me jump!" I laughed. "Yes, I'm fine, this is a lovely room."

Laurie came in, pushed the door to and enveloped me in a bear hug. "And you, Miss Christopher, are even lovelier!"

"You all right, you two? Dinner will be ready soon!"

I giggled as Mrs Walker's voice floated up from downstairs.

"Is this room bugged?" I whispered.

"I wouldn't put it past her," Laurie grinned as he gave me a lingering kiss.

I kissed him back, then asked, "So, what is a Bonfire Carol Service when it's at home?"

"It's like firework night, but with carols instead of fireworks."

"And they burn King Herod instead of Guy Fawkes?"

Laurie chuckled, "I don't think so, although until recently we had a dreadful vicar. A few of us lads from the church choir would have happily burned an effigy of him in our younger days."

"You? A choirboy? You were never serious enough, surely?" I teased.

"I was a very angelic young lad, I'll have you know."

"An image which broke with your voice, I suppose?"

"Where that vicar was concerned, us lads were little devils, I admit, but he deserved the tricks we played on him."

The stairs creaked outside the bedroom door, a polite knock and Alf popped his head round.

"You talking about the Reverend Passwith? Goodness, but he was a bit of a so–... er, so-and-so."

I smiled at Alf's discretion. "What was so awful about him?"

Laurie frowned, "He was a disgruntled misery who preached 'thou shalt not steal' every autumn and dropped us boys in the proverbial do-do whenever we were caught scrumping apples. Which was quite often."

I didn't comment that us girls were as capable at apple scrumping.

"He was rather a holier-than-thou person," Alf added, "always poking his nose into other peoples' business. But you're aware that he retired and moved away around the same time you left for London, Laurie? I don't think anyone in the village has missed him, though there's been a fair bit of gossip about him this past week or so."

Laurie's frown deepened. "Gossip, Dad, can be dangerous. It's rarely accurate."

Alf grinned. "Gossip can be interesting in a small place like this, son, but, as it happens, it's true. His wife disappeared in early May, then he retired, shut the cottage up and left. But he moved back ten days ago – with a woman." Alf tapped the side of his nose, "A woman who is younger than himself, and who is not his wife."

"What? Really?" Laurie was surprised. "And him a vicar an' all!"

"She might be his sister or a housekeeper," I suggested. "An explanation doesn't have to be anything sordid or smutty."

Alf chuckled. "Quite right, my dear girl, quite right, but that hypothesis isn't as gossip-worthy, is it? Whoever, or whatever, she is, I suppose he can do as he likes – within the letter of the law, that is. Mind you, no one knows what happened to *Mrs* Passwith." He scrunched up his face and made a lurid strangling motion with his hands, whispered in a sinister voice, "Perhaps he mur...d...ered her!"

He noticed my stricken face as I remembered the ghastly murder that Laurie and I had discovered back in the summer.

"I *am* only joking, my dear." He patted my shoulder

and changed the subject. "Anyway, I've been ordered to tell you that Dinner Is About To Be Served."

He offered me his arm and escorted me down the stairs and into the dining room which was through one of the doors in the hall. Another, I later discovered, opened onto Alf's office, his personal domain, which looked out over the valley. He was a self-employed successful and sought after accountant, although Laurie said he spent most of his time in there sprawled in the leather armchair reading fiction or travel books.

The dining room was a lovely old, atmospheric room oozing the charm of past history. Alf ceremoniously escorted me to my seat at a rather splendid mahogany table that could easily seat ten people, and poured me a glass of red wine, as if I were visiting royalty.

I liked Alf, I had a feeling that we were going to be good friends.

3

BONFIRE HEAT AND A COLD FROST

The eight-foot-high bonfire had been built on the village green, and was well ablaze by the time we got there. Laurie had told me to wrap up warm, so I'd donned my duffle coat, gloves and faux fur hat – which looked more like a curled-up grey cat than a hat – modest length tweed skirt, cashmere jumper and my walking shoes with woolly socks over my tights. Standing near the blaze, Laurie's arm around my waist, I wasn't feeling the cold, despite the glisten of frost and the clouds of breath from everyone who had gathered to sing carols.

Sitting under a protective awning on bales of blanket-covered straw, was a group of enthusiastic musicians, consisting of an accordion, a guitar and a fiddle player. They had started the evening off by launching into a rousing rendition of *In Dulci Jubilo*, although I don't know how their hands hadn't immediately frozen, despite the fingerless woolly gloves they wore. Following on, we sang several joyful carols, *Good King Wenceslas, While Shepherds Watched, O Come All Ye Faithful* and a couple more, then we had a break for mulled wine or beer, hot sausage rolls kept warm on dishes propped over paraffin camping stoves, and mince pies – not that I was hungry after the huge dinner Mrs W had served; even so, I managed two of each, which, being home-made, were delicious.

"Did you know that 'bonfire' comes from an old word for 'bone fire', where the ancient people used to burn bones?" I said to Laurie through a mouthful of pastry crumbs.

"What, like cave men and such?"

"No, I think the Celts or Iron Age people," I frowned, then laughed, "Uncle Toby told me, but I can't remember everything he said now."

"Well, I hope he meant animal bones, not human remains!" Alf chuckled, overhearing.

"Actually," I answered, my face blushing slightly, although I don't think it noticed because of the heat emitting from the flames, "I think he *did* mean human – you know, sacrifice and all that."

Alf frowned, thoughtfully. "Sacrificed dead or alive, that's the question! Maybe a winter solstice custom – appropriate, eh?" His frown changed to a grin. "Shortest night was last night, well, technically, the early hours of this morning, so I reckon we're near enough for old rituals. Who do you suggest we toss onto the fire? My money would be on Gran, Laurie, if she were here. Or Haywood over there?"

I rather wished I hadn't brought the subject up. Laurie's dad was only joking, but he had consumed several beers and his voice was rather loud as he nodded towards a dishevelled man standing slightly apart from the crowd over to one side, an almost empty pint glass of beer in his hand. A girl, I reckoned to be about my own age of eighteen, stood next to him, her puckered expression sour. Both of them were glowering in our direction – they couldn't have heard Alf, could they?

"Another mince pie?" Laurie asked me, swiftly changing the subject.

"I shouldn't but, yes, please."

"And another mulled wine?"

I said yes to that, too.

Laurie left me with Alf, who steered me nearer the fire as the 'orchestra' started up again, leading us all into a triumphant rendition of *Hark The Herald Angels*. Mrs Walker, I noticed, was gossiping with a group of ladies who kept surreptitiously glancing towards me. Summing me up, I supposed, wondering if I was suitable or worthy to be 'Lawrence's' girlfriend.

The carol changed to the gentler *Away In A Manger*. I wondered where Laurie had got to. There had been a short queue at the refreshments stall, but it had dwindled now, and he wasn't there. Then I saw him talking to the man Alf had called Haywood, who was on his own now, the girl having disappeared. The man was waving his arms about in an angry, animated fashion, then he jabbed his finger into Laurie's shoulder. Laurie's expression was as angry. It had obviously been an altercation of some sort, but he brushed his assailant aside, spun on his heel and walked away – back to the refreshment stall. A moment later, he was at my side, handing me a glass of warm, spiced wine and a mince pie.

"Sorry I took so long," he apologised, "had to go to the loo over in the village hall."

"Who was that man?" I asked, after taking a sip of the aromatic wine.

"What man?"

"The one who was arguing with you. The one who looked like he could do with a shave and a decent set of clothes?"

"Oh, *that* man. Godfrey Haywood. He's the tenant of the smallholding at the top of the lane."

"The place that looks like it's falling to pieces? Higher Valley View?"

"That's the one."

"He looks about as rough as his farm."

"He is."

"So what was he arguing about?" Pulling teeth would have been easier than trying to get a coherent answer!

"Moaning about the state of the fencing along the lane. It's habitual for him to complain about it, although it's *his* fencing, *his* responsibility. His livestock is always breaking it down because he doesn't mend it properly, but he always hopes that he can bully Dad into doing the repairs and footing the bill, on account of the lane having shared access."

"He's got the grumps this time," Alf added, joining in, "because I gave him the heave-ho from doing our gardening a week ago. Apart from the fact that there's not much to do this time of year, he frequently never turned up, and, when he did bother, he barely managed any actual gardening. I asked him to spread some of the compost heap on the vegetable beds, but he was worse the wear for drink and trailed most of it along the path – left it for me to tidy up. I might as well have done it myself in the first place. Final straw and all that. I told him not to come again."

Then the girl re-appeared. I watched her stride across the green from the direction of the village hall, her face like God's wrath turned to hardened lard, heading straight for us.

As the crowd was bursting into *God Rest Ye Merry Gentlemen*, Laurie stepped forward to meet the girl, his arm outstretched, palm raised in a 'stop' gesture, as if he were a traffic cop not a newly qualified Detective Sergeant.

"So, you've found the nerve to come back, then?"

the girl sneered. She flung a crude gesture towards me. "And you brought a fancy London tart, too? How dare you! You swan off with my sister, and not a word from either of you since? Where is she? Eh? What have you done with Colly? You'd better come clean, Lawrence Walker, or I'll be telling what I know. I'll tell it all!"

I instantly had a few similar questions of my own rattling around in my head. Who was this young woman? What was it she knew? Who was her sister, this 'Colly' person?

And what did both of them have to do with my Laurie?

4

INTERLUDE: LAURIE

It was love at first sight when I met Jan, although I kept telling myself that such things never happened in real life, but by the time I had known her for over a week – and we had waded through the sordid circumstances of the rather nasty murder of an elderly lady – I knew my feelings were fact, and dared to hope that they were, or at least, might, come to be reciprocated. Inviting her to spend Christmas with my folks, though, could have been one of my more ill-thought ideas, but I truly did not want to spend Christmas without her, and I knew that my parents expected me to go home for the festivities. Mum would have been so hurt had I stayed in London.

Dad was all right, even if he tended to get a little 'jolly' after he'd had one too many. Mum was, well, Mum was Mum. She liked everything to be respectable in front of the neighbours and visitors, 'keep up with the Joneses' type of thing. Which was ironic, as her mother's maiden name had been Jones. Mum took things too seriously, a glass half-empty person. I often wished, even when I'd been a naïve teenager, that she could understand that an empty glass could be refilled, and that she should see more of the funny side of things, let her hair down, enjoy life, rather than worry on silly annoyances which were not particularly important.

I'd realised as I reached maturity, however, that her fussing was because of anxiety and a lack of self-confidence. This need to prove everything was tickety-boo in order to appear capable had been a part of her life ever since she was little. Her mother, Grandma Brigham, had not been around much in those childhood years, Mum being brought up until she was thirteen by her maternal grandparents – the Joneses.

Old Mr Jones had been a Northumbrian shipbuilder and one of the men who had joined the famous workers' rebellion Jarrow March to London in 1936, but he and his wife had been killed outright by a German bombing raid in April 1941. I think Mum always felt guilty that she had survived and they did not. She had been staying with a friend outside of town and the incident had meant that she then had to join her mother, who lived and worked during the war near what is now the New Town of Milton Keynes. From what I gather, that joining had been something of an inconvenient nuisance for both of them, but Gran in particular.

For myself, the matter of Chloë and Colette Haywood was also an inconvenient nuisance, and I could tell by Jan's face when Chloë vented her public rant, that I would have some explaining to do.

I had been enjoying the carols around the bonfire, the event was always congenial, especially after a few drinks had been sampled. The village coven of the Women's Institute provided the food, which was on sale with all profits going to a local charity. 'Coven', I must point out, was my own private term; they were all nice ladies really, if maybe a little organising, and old fashioned in the prudish sense. Ladies with 1950s moral standards, and skirt lengths to match.

Godfrey Haywood had indulged in more beer than was good for him when he accosted me to grumble about the fencing, which, despite his protestations, was his problem, not ours. Dad had given him the elbow from the gardening job, so he complained about that, and then went on to rant about the disappearance of his eldest daughter, Colette. She was my age, twenty-five, our May birthdays being within a day of each other. I had gone out with her for a few weeks earlier in the year – 'gone out' in the sense of having a couple of drinks together in the village pub and to the cinema in Barnstaple once, and that was only because I felt sorry for her. Her mother had gone off with someone else when Colette was seventeen, Chloë, only ten. Mr Haywood had expected his eldest to step into the shoes of being cook, cleaner and housekeeper regardless of an opportunity for her to go to college or start a career. I often wondered, perhaps uncharitably, that he'd also expected certain other 'wifely' duties, although Colly had never made any hint of such an abuse. All I knew was that there was a smallholding to run and a father and younger sister to care for. They were a wild pair, the girls, but frankly, Mr Haywood taking no interest in their education didn't matter, both of them had rarely attended school.

I went to college, then university for a short while, but it wasn't for me; I left after two terms, and went into the police force instead. It was only after coming across Colette walking, alone, along a dark Devon lane back in March one wet night, that I asked her out.

I had been on my way home from an eventful shift, and she fell in front of my car. Literally. She'd tripped and fallen down like an expertly bowled skittle. I jammed on the brakes, picked her up, put her in the passenger seat, wrapped her in a blanket and dropped her home. She was in a state: soaked through, her stockings laddered. I didn't ask what had happened, but I didn't need to as I put two-and-two together and came up with a pretty reasonable four.

We'd arrested her boyfriend that same evening for a burglary where an old man had been brutally beaten, £10 and his pension book stolen. To the boyfriend's misfortune, a neighbour had called the police after seeing and recognising him as he'd scuttled away from the old man's house. Less than an hour later, we apprehended the thief as he tried to squeeze out through his own ground floor window – the window being small, he being large of belly and beam. The idiot had managed to get himself stuck. My PC colleague and I pulled him free, cuffed him to his own bedframe, and found quite a few interesting stolen items in his room, including a wad of money and a pension book; both of which later proved to have the old man's fingerprints on them.

I was sure that there had been someone else in that one-room bed-sit: her cheap jasmine perfume lingered, there were two cups and used plates in the small corner sink; a brassiere tangled in with the unmade bed sheets. Unlike her boyfriend, she had been slender enough to slip out through the window. We had no way of knowing who the girl was, nor any proof that she'd had any connection with the robbery.

Colette was officially questioned the next day, for she'd been seen with this piece of slime on several occasions, but she claimed that she'd finished with him a week beforehand. We had no reason to doubt her. Her fingerprints were all over the bedsit, but she hadn't denied being there during the previous week, so we had to discount that evidence.

I knew she was lying. I knew she had been there

with her boyfriend that evening, but I had also been convinced that the burglary was nothing to do with Colly.

When I helped her into my car after her fall, despite the drenching, she still reeked of the same sickly perfume. Not conclusive, but I guessed she'd managed to climb out of the bedsit window with the intention of beating a hasty retreat. She admitted to me, when I asked, that she had been in Barnstaple at a pub, waiting for a friend who hadn't turned up, had then taken the last train and was walking home from Umberleigh station. All of three miles, much of it up several very steep hills, in the rain and the dark. I don't know if it was good or bad fortune that I'd come across her halfway up one of those hills.

Her involvement with the robbery would have been circumstantial, with no proof of evidence, or so my DCI, back at the police station, would have said had I mentioned my theory. So I kept it to myself. I did check her story about being in the pub and catching the last train – pub landlord and station master both confirmed she was telling the truth. But then, both these sightings had occurred *after* we had arrived at the boyfriend's bedsit. Still, I gave her the benefit of the doubt.

I asked her out a few days later because I was on my own, at a loose end, and I felt sorry for her. I made it clear, however, that I was due to leave for London soon after my birthday. I was transferring there in order to further my detective experience and do more with my required forthcoming sergeant's exams. North Devon does not have a high crime rate for anything really interesting. Burglaries, motoring offences, drunk and disorderly, sheep and cattle rustling... A couple of grisly murders in a couple of decades, one of the most notorious being during the war when a Bideford farmer was shot and his body was consumed by his pigs. Add to that, the DS I had worked with was lazy, and the DCI, although a nice guy, was old fashioned, due for retirement and, consequently, not very dedicated to his job. I was learning nothing from either of them, except how to file reports and dodge as much work as possible.

All the same, in hindsight, I should never have become involved with Colette Haywood. Especially when she asked if she could come to London with me. I said no, but I did offer to run her to the station – an offer which she refused in no uncertain, unladylike terms, but changed her mind on the day I left.

She was waiting for me at the top of the lane, a duffle-bag of meagre belongings and a red plastic handbag being her only luggage. I repeated that I could not take her to London. As it happened, I was not making a direct journey, but was staying *en route* with a friend in Swindon for a couple of days first. I dropped her at Umberleigh station, even though it was a little out of my way, gave her a generous £5 note, and wished her all the best. I never saw her again.

But how was I to explain all that to Jan?

5

NOISES IN THE NIGHT

My fault, I hadn't realised how potent that mulled wine had been. I wasn't drunk when we got back to the house, but I was a little on the wrong side of sober. I hadn't spoken to Laurie all the way back – we'd gone in his dad's car because it is larger than Laurie's and the village is more than a mile from the house, and while the lane is walkable during the day, at night the mud and ruts can be hazardous, even with the aid of torches. I sat in the back of the car with Mrs Walker, my arms folded, peering at the blackness outside the window. I wasn't cross that Laurie'd had a previous girlfriend, it would have been surprising if he hadn't for he was very good looking – he resembled a young Cary Grant. But it did irk that he was clearly not being quite truthful to me about that girl.

When we got home, I announced that I was going straight to bed, said goodnight, and went up. Ignoring Laurie.

I heard Mrs Walker whisper, in the sort of whisper that would have carried several miles in a thunderstorm, "Have you two had a tiff, pet?"

Laurie was better at keeping his voice low, so I

didn't hear his reply.

I crawled into bed and huddled under the eiderdown, cuddling Bee Bear, miserable and unable to sleep. I heard the floorboards creak along the landing, and then 'my' stairs, followed by a light tap on my door.

"Jan? Are you awake? Can I come in?"

Laurie. I made no answer.

"Jan?"

The door opened slightly, the light from the hall streaming in. "Jan?"

I lay still, deliberately keeping my breathing low and even. He didn't come in, just stood at the threshold.

"Night, night, sweetheart. Sleep tight." The door began to close, but before it clicked shut I heard Laurie whisper, "I love you. I've been an ass. Sorry."

I turned over, sat up, feeling a right heel, but the door had shut and embarrassment swamped through me. What I *should* have done was run after him, but the moment had passed. Aunt Madge always told me that the secret of a good marriage was to never go to bed as Mr and Mrs Grump – always kiss and make up before going to sleep, even if you have to cross your fingers while saying 'sorry'. But Laurie and I were not a married couple, and it was beginning to dawn on me that, despite going out with him for just over five months, I didn't really *know* him. Going for a drink, to a disco, to the pictures or a restaurant; enjoying his company for an evening, a day out, an intimate weekend, none of that was the same as being together in a home environment – *his* home environment

A strip of light squeezed under the door, then that went out. I lay in bed, hugging Bee Bear and listening to the sounds of the house settling for the night – the people within and the old building itself. I heard the grandfather clock prematurely strike midnight. Ten minutes left, in actual time, to follow my aunt's advice. Should I get up? Tiptoe to Laurie's room? Unsure what to do, I did nothing. The clock chimed the quarter-hour. Too late now. Today had become yesterday.

I must have dozed, for a tawny owl hooting, long and loud right outside, woke me up just as the clock downstairs struck one. I smiled, wondered if a mouse had run up and down, as in Hickory-Dickory-Dock. The owl hooted again. I'd seen plenty of pictures of owls, starting when I was little with *Little Grey Rabbit* and Beatrix Potter's stories – who could forget Squirrel Nutkin's mishap with the owl! So I knew exactly what a tawny owl would look like, but I had never actually *seen* a real one.

As the bedroom was at the end of the house it had three large windows on each outside wall, so, even with the curtains partially closed, I could see quite adequately because of the full moon. I got out of bed and hurried to the middle, biggest window, which had a velvet-padded window seat. I pulled the curtains aside and peered out.

The silvery moonlit view sloped steeply away from the house for about half-a-mile, down towards the River Taw, then rose again on the other side in rounded hills of rich, lush, farmland that was ideal for cattle and sheep. Frost sparkled beneath the star-twinkling sky. The trees, bare of leaf, were stark against the skyline, the hedgerows dark, casting long, black shadows. I heard the owl again coming from one of the oak trees along the lane. Despite the cold, I opened the window, leaned out.

There was something ethereal about the owl's call, not scary, but exciting. Maybe because owls encapsulated the world of the night, the topsy-turvy, back-to-front opposite of our own daytime existence? I caught my breath; the bird glided silently across the garden, its body dark against the moonlight, its shadow flickering over the ground beneath. It was bigger than I had expected. I had never seen anything so utterly beautiful before!

Then I saw something else moving between the vegetable plots, large and black... Two crouched shapes, slowly edging along the path. I opened the window wider, shivered against the blast of cold air as I leaned further out, listening. Something was making a sort of wheezing, snuffling sound. A burglar with asthma? Frightened, I closed the window, rushed back to the bed, shoved my feet into my slippers and threw my dressing gown round my shoulders. Mrs Walker had left a torch on the bedside table in case I needed one, so I grabbed it and switched it on.

The floorboards creaked as if a herd of elephants were thundering through the house, but I didn't care. I ran, as fast as furry mule slippers permitted, so a sort of hobbling, shuffle, down the stairs and along the landing to Laurie's room, where I barged the door open.

"Laurie!" Not a shout, but definitely not a whisper. "Laurie! There are two burglars in the garden!"

He was up, out of bed and running to my room. Alf appeared at his bedroom door, pulling a tartan woollen dressing gown on over his striped pyjamas.

Laurie's mum, her voice muffled from within the room; "What is it? What has happened?"

"Stay there!" Laurie ordered as he disappeared through the doorway of my bedroom. Neither Alf nor myself obeyed, we followed. I turned round as the landing light behind us snapped on, to see Mrs W, her hair in curlers beneath a bright pink hairnet, appear in our wake.

"Turn the light off!" I hissed. "There are burglars

outside!" Not that a light mattered, the noise we were making would have alerted them anyway.

Then Laurie and Alf, who was beside him peering out of the window, both roared with laughter.

"It's OK," Laurie guffawed, "put the light on. It's only two of Haywood's pigs!"

Mrs W pushed past me, her unfastened candlewick dressing gown ballooning behind her like an Elizabethan cape, showing her ankle-length blue, winceyette nightie beneath it.

"What?" she shrieked as she rushed to the window. "The garden? What are they doing in the garden? Lawrence, Alfred, don't stand there like gormless nincompoops, get down there and chase them out! That wretched man. He never tends his fences. How did they get in? Was our gate closed?" She looked accusingly one-by-one at us. "Who was last in?"

"I was," Laurie confessed, "I gave Bess a run up the lane, remember? The gate was properly latched behind me when we got back, I heard it click."

"Well, it's obviously open now. They couldn't have got through the hedge, it's too solid, and, anyway, there's a wire fence running through the middle of it," Alf declared.

Mrs W leaned out of the window and flapped a handkerchief towards the two pigs which were rooting at a flower bed alongside the house.

"Shoo! Shoo! Go on, go away, you nasty things! Oh, my roses! My beautiful roses, they're grubbing them all up!" She turned away from the window and sat, slumped and crumpled on the end of my bed, tears cascading down her face. Laurie tried to console her, but she shrugged him off.

Alf gestured towards the door. "Come on, son, get some clothes and boots on, we'd best evict the boogers before they do too much damage."

33

"I'll look after her," I offered, smiling at Laurie. "I'll make us a cup of tea."

He nodded and blew me a kiss from the door.

I blew one back and hoped he realised the conveyed message. All was forgiven. At least, it was for now.

I managed to bumble my way around the kitchen. Fortunately, there was a Russell Hobbs electric kettle, although I could have negotiated the Aga if I'd put my mind to it, as we had one at home. By exploring cupboards, I found cups, tea, some biscuits, and carried a tray up to Mrs W who was anxiously watching her husband and son from the now closed window.

I peeped out as I handed her the tea. Laurie and Alf were, not very successfully, trying to shoosh both pigs out through a second gate which led into the field beyond, using garden brooms to chivvy them along, except neither pig had the slightest intention of being chivvied. There was a lot of encouraging yelling from the two men, and a good bit of indignant *oink-oinking* from the pigs. Actually, there was some oinking from Alf and Laurie as well. I assume it was their version of talking piggy language. It didn't seem to be working.

I giggled.

Laurie's mum looked at me with an expression that resembled a schoolmistress who had just discovered something small, furry and very unpleasantly dead in her desk drawer.

"Those pigs have destroyed my garden," she said, her voice wobbling towards more tears. "It is not amusing."

I suppose it wasn't. Not really, but it wasn't easy to *not* laugh. I bit my lip, held my breath as I stared out of the window. Alf was pushing the larger of the pigs through the open gateway, the brush of his broom very firmly anchored to its round, pink bottom. He gave a shove and the pig, having had enough of spiky bristles prickling its backside, suddenly darted forward. The other pig, seeing its friend disappear into the night, wobbled after it at an ungainly trot. I had no idea that pigs could move so fast when they wanted to. Neither, it appeared, did Alf, for he lost his balance and fell into the hedge, his broom jabbing into it as if he were a knight jousting with the holly and hawthorn.

I couldn't help it, I laughed outright. "Don Quixote strikes again! Although I thought he had a donkey, not Pinky and Perky."

Mrs W stared at me over her tea cup for a moment. "If you are going to use analogies of TV puppets," she said in a very bland voice, "wouldn't that be Muffin the Mule, not a donkey?" Then she snorted, burst into laughter and patted my hand. "Oh, Jan pet, you are a breath of fresh air. I'm so glad Lawrence invited you here."

On impulse I hugged her – minding the tea cup. I was used to my Aunt Madge's sense of humour, and her frequent hugs, but had the impression that Mrs W wasn't that much of a 'hug' person, but to my surprise, she hugged me, one-handed, back.

"I love my son dearly,' she said, "but none of his girlfriends have ever seemed, well, suitable." She paused, blushed, admitted, "Oh dear, that sounded somewhat rude."

"Not really," I replied, "until now, Aunt Madge has always said the same about my poor taste in friends, boy *or* girl. In hindsight, where most of them were concerned, I heartily agree with her."

"I'd best put that kettle on again," Mrs W said, getting to her feet, "they'll both be like walking icebergs when they come in. Fresh hot water bottles for the beds, too. Do you want one?"

I wasn't sure if she meant tea or a hot water bottle. In the end, I had both.

6

THE SCENT OF ROSES

(MASKED BY BACON)

The next morning was crisp but clear, with the leaves of trees and hedges white-frosted, and the sky above, a pale-washed blue. The river, down in the valley, was shrouded in skeins of mist that rolled along the dip between the hills, making it seem that the fields and trees on the far side of the valley were floating in mid-air. I opened a bedroom window and filled my lungs with the clean, damp smells of the unpolluted countryside, then peered down into the garden to see what damage the pigs had done. Alf was already up and dressed at the far end of the path, making a start on tidying up. From what I could see, there was a lot of muck spread everywhere – earth and pig poo – rooted up plants and several broken garden canes.

Pigs, so Laurie had told me last night, (*very* early hours of the morning!) over cups of tea in the kitchen, are 'rooters', they grub for food by digging in the soil with their snouts, eating through anything in the way – roots, brambles, whatever they come across. Apparently, they can clear overgrown land in no time – nature's ploughs, leaving not a trace beyond bare earth and their droppings. I always thought that all pigs ate were kitchen scraps and acorns. (Thanks to an upbringing on Winnie the Pooh and Piglet!)

"They have powerful jaws," Alf had explained. "If they find a dead body, a rabbit, fox, pheasant, badger – a deer – they can strip what they find down to the bone, even crunching up the smaller bones and eating them as well."

I wasn't sure if he had been pulling my leg, but as far as the 'rooting' was concerned, I could see with my own eyes that he had told the truth. Mrs W's roses had been well and truly dug up from their beds alongside the wall of the house. Alf had gathered them together and put them in a bucket, and although I knew little about gardening, I guessed they would not be replanted for some while. Put them back now, and they would die from frostbite.

The nip in the air was a bit too cold for leaning out of a window for too long in my pyjamas – even though they were soft and fluffy, and very pink, which matched my room nicely, but did little for my rapidly freezing fingers and toes. I washed quickly at the handbasin and brushed my teeth, dressed in jeans and jumper, my hair scrunched into a ponytail, and hurried downstairs to where I could smell the waft of frying bacon.

"Good morning!" I said as I entered the kitchen. "Mm, that smells delicious."

Mrs W turned away from the Aga to smile at me. "I hope sausage, egg and bacon is alright for you, Jan pet? Did you sleep all right after the..." she gulped, hesitated, "after the pigs?" There came a little choked sob in her throat.

I crossed the stone flagged floor quickly and slid my arm round her waist.

"Don't upset yourself too much," I said, trying to cheer her up, "roses are dormant in winter, aren't they?

And I noticed yesterday that you've already pruned them down nicely. The roots have been exposed, but one night probably won't harm them. As long as we get them tucked up warm and cosy as soon as we can, they'll be as good as new come the spring."

I sounded more optimistic than I felt, but I remembered a similar situation at home when Aunt Madge had discovered three of her precious rose bushes had been dug up by next-door's errant dog. A huge shaggy thing that was as big as a haystack, and looked like one as well.

"She's right," Laurie said, coming through the door from the scullery beyond, and shutting it quickly behind him. The scullery, I had discovered last night, gave access to the garden and housed old coats, boots, mops, buckets and brooms, a twin-tub washing machine, refrigerator and a large, modern deep freezer – even we didn't have one of *those* at home! Laurie's face was red-cheeked from the cold outside, his feet clad only in socks. He had a basket of eggs in his hand, which he put on the top of one of the kitchen units.

"Your hens are laying well, Mum, despite the cold; I've let them all out," he said as he crossed the kitchen and retrieved a pair of leather moccasin slippers from beside the lower oven of the Aga where they had been keeping warm. I noticed another pair there as well; Alf's, I assumed.

"And what would you know about roses?" Mrs W said to him with a slight scoff of derision. "The nearest you ever got to gardening was picking the peas and raspberries when they were ready, and eating most of them."

"Dad told me the same as Jan just said," Laurie answered, giving his mum a kiss on her cheek. "He's taking them up to the greenhouse where he'll pot them into compost and keep them there, safe, until they can be replanted. No great harm done."

"Is there a garden centre anywhere near?" I asked. "Perhaps you could also get some nice new ones?"

"Good idea!" Laurie answered, approving, "and we'll send the bill to him up the lane! Any tea in the pot?" He went to the table, felt beneath the tea cosy. "Want one, Jan?"

"Yes, please, but shall I lay the table in the dining room first, Mrs W?" I thought I ought to offer, make myself useful.

"Certainly not," she responded, "you are our guest. You sit yourself down; Lawrence will do it – but we eat breakfast here in the kitchen." She paused, suddenly uncertain. "Will that be all right, we can use the dining room if you prefer?"

Did she think I was ultra posh or something? Dinner of an evening with a group of companionable friends or family was nice in the setting of a dining room, but breakfast didn't need that sort of formality.

"The kitchen's fine," I said, "more friendly."

"Gran will expect the dining room for breakfast, lunch, afternoon tea, dinner *and* supper," Laurie remarked, opening a drawer and selecting knives and forks.

"Well, she can expect all she wants, but she isn't getting it. Tomato ketchup and HP brown sauce are in the larder, Lawrence, and Jan pet, please, call me Elsie."

That was a relief; calling her 'Mrs W' made me think of Aunt Madge's twice-weekly cleaning lady, Mrs P. Her name was Mrs Pembleton, and she was lovely, but, unfortunately, she had a slight bladder problem and occasionally whiffed a wee bit of, well, pee. We never let on to anyone that the P wasn't short for her name.

"Did you know," I said, sitting down at the table

and accepting the cup of tea Laurie had poured for me, "that HP stands for 'Houses of Parliament' as supposedly it was used in the restaurant there, back in the 1900s?"

Mrs W – Elsie – laughed as she dished up the breakfasts. "I didn't know there *was* a restaurant there!"

"Ma!" Laurie groaned, rolling his eyes, "you surely don't expect Prime Minister Mr Heath and all the MPs to take little paper bags of sandwiches into the House of Commons for their lunch, do you?"

Actually, it would probably be evening dinner, as I thought the Commons sat of an evening, but I didn't want to say so, in case I was wrong.

"Of course, I don't," Elsie sniffed as she reached for the brown sauce, "I would expect them to have proper little lunch boxes – like that battered old red one the Chancellor carries to work on Budget Day."

For a moment I wondered if she was serious. Until she burst out laughing.

7

TO MARKET, TO MARKET

(BUT NOT TO BUY A FAT PIG. WE'D HAD ENOUGH OF THOSE!)

South Molton Pannier Market was a real treat. I'd never seen anything like it, nor had I heard of Pannier Markets, but then, they are special to the West Country and Devon in particular. As a Londoner, the nearest I'd come to such a thing was the mile long Walthamstow High Street and all the traders' stalls set out on each side of the road: an enjoyable shopping experience in nice weather, but in the rain or cold wind? No thanks. The Pannier Market was under cover, built behind the impressive old Guildhall, so much more civilised.

Laurie, as much of a mine of information as is my Uncle Toby on occasion, told me as we drove into town after breakfast, that *pannier* was French for *basket*, so really it was a basket market, but in this instance it meant goods brought to market *in* baskets by farmers, not a market that sold baskets. Although, there *was* a basket stall among the dozens of others selling fruit, vegetables, meat pies and Devon Pasties (baked in a different shape to the *Cornish* Pasty). Cakes, fresh-baked bread, cheeses, meats... Then there were the Christmas stalls gay with festive decorations, cards, children's toys, Christmas foods. To my eyes, it seemed like an Aladdin's Cave of delightful paraphernalia. I inspected a beautiful, exquisitely carved wooden tawny owl sitting on a tree stump. He was about six inches high and gorgeous, but I thought £3 was expensive, as my monthly salary was just over £100, so, only £25 a week, and a quarter of that went to Aunt Madge for my share of board and lodging. Then there were bus fares to and from work, clothes, make-up. It didn't go far, I can tell you. Reluctantly, I smiled at the stall holder and moved on. One stall had an array of sweet-scented hyacinths growing in gayly painted bowls. I bought a pink one and a blue one for Elsie, then moved on to a book stall further up the aisle while Laurie took the plants and the other things we'd purchased back to the car – Elsie had sent us off with a vast shopping list of last-minute essentials.

You would think that, working in a library, I'd be glad to get away from books for a while, but not so! I enjoy browsing bookstalls and bookshops. It is compulsive, almost addictive, and I always have to buy at least *one* book. I pounced on one that I noticed on the stall, *Dune* by Frank Herbert, enthralling science fiction which I owned, but only in paperback. This was a hardback first edition. I *had* to have it, and at thirty new pence, was just within my budget. I wrote science fiction myself with the probably hopeless ambition of one day completing a novel and having it published. I had my characters, plot and over fifty thousand words typed out, but I was well aware that I'd be very lucky if any publishing house would even look at it, when, *if*, I ever finished it. Although I did often remind myself that *Dune* had been rejected by over twenty publishing houses before Chilton Books picked it up. It went on to win the prestigious Nebula *and* Hugo awards. So there was, perhaps, hope for my small effort? You can't say I'm not an optimist!

I then spotted something else; a leather-bound photograph album, lovingly filled with photographs of exotic foreign places. Beneath each, a short, handwritten description: *'The Taj Mahal, India. Evocative, romantic and beautiful, visit at dawn or dusk, you will not regret the sight of those exquisite, painted skies.'*

The same woman was in most of the photos, the photographer's wife, perhaps? In the first part of the album she was quite young and dressed in the post-World War One 1920s style of low-waisted dresses, with a bobbed hairstyle beneath a variety of cloche hats. She wore scarves in most of the pictures, with bold, striking Art Deco geometric designs, which were probably brightly coloured, but as these were black-and-white photos, it was hard to tell. Further on, the woman was dressed in a uniform – ATS, the Auxiliary Territorial Service? WRAF, the Women's Royal Air Force? I wasn't sure of the difference, and the photos were too small for me to see the badges she wore. One photo was of her with another woman and two men who wore smart suits and rosebud buttonholes. A wedding photo. The bride was dressed in a white jacket over a lace-trimmed frock, and carried a posy of flowers. Beyond the date, 1945, there were no names or description beneath. A post-war wedding, then, probably not enough clothing coupons to warrant a proper wedding dress. My Aunt Madge had married Uncle Toby in October 1945, her dress had been silk, handmade from a reclaimed parachute that had been dyed an attractive ivory colour. I'd seen it often, as she kept it wrapped in brown paper in a box on top of one of her wardrobes.

I peered through the crowd to see if Laurie was coming back, spotted him, and was about to wave when I saw that he had stopped to talk to a young woman. *That* young woman, Chloë Haywood. She seemed in a better mood today, for there was no arm waving or apparent shouting, just conversation. She laid her hand on his shoulder. He leant forward, kissed her cheek. She kissed him back. On the lips. I didn't know what to think. Was that him being friendly, or was there something more between them?

When he joined me at the stall, I said nothing about the encounter. Neither did he. I didn't mention the trace of her lipstick on his mouth, either.

Laurie cradled his arm around my waist and gave me a kiss. I moved away from him slightly, pretending that I was embarrassed. I didn't want to taste her lipstick.

"Look," I said, changing the 'subject' as it were, and showed him the album. "Would your dad like this?"

Not noticing that anything was amiss, nor making any mention of Chloë, Laurie took it from me and leafed through.

"You told me that he loves books about travel," I said, pointing to another photograph of the Acropolis in Athens.

Laurie was nodding. "Yes, Dad has always wanted to travel, but Mum won't go any further than Bournemouth, so his wanderings are all in his mind – and pictures in books." He flicked through the pages again, there was no indication of who the album had belonged to.

"Do thee knows an'thin' 'bout she?" Laurie asked the stallholder in broad Devonian. I thought he was talking about Chloë for a moment, then realised that Devonians referred to objects as 'he' or 'she'.

The stallholder shook his head. "I 'as 'er vrom some'un who doos 'ouse clearance up Tivvy way. Vive shillin' an' sixp'nce an' she be yourn.'

We had gone decimal, changing from £ S D some months ago, but a lot of folk still used 'old money'. I attempted a quick conversion in my head, but Laurie was quicker.

"She be old vo'graphs, no much use to 'air nor 'ide be she? I'll give'n thee two bob ver 'er."

I hid a smile; unlike the stout, grey-haired gentleman behind his stall, Laurie usually only had a very mild Devonshire accent, but in bargaining mode, he was putting in all the dialect he could muster.

The stallholder frowned, assuming that Laurie was local and not, like me, an out-of-town tourist – a 'grockle' as they called us down here. He sniffed, said, "Four." (Only the f sounded like v – so, 'vor'.

"Three. Las' ovver."

"Done."

My hasty recalculation made that 15p. A bargain!

Laurie looked at his watch as I tucked our prizes under my arm.

"We'd better get our skates on," Laurie said, "we've got to get to Umberleigh to meet Gran off the train. She'll grumble if we keep her waiting." He paused, tilted his head to one side. "You Ok? That album was a good find. Well done, you!"

I mentally pulled myself together. I was being silly, making mountains out of molehills about Chloë. "I'm fine. A bit tired from last night. Had we better get Grumbling Gran some hyacinths as well, do you think? Will she mind if she doesn't have the same as your mum?"

"Good point," he acknowledged, "she *will* mind, although I can guarantee she'll claim that flowers are a waste of money."

We threaded our way back through the Christmas crowd and purchased two more scented blooms, then hurried to the rear entrance and the car park. A few yards before we reached the slope leading out through the open doors, a man stepped purposefully into our path. Godfrey Haywood. Was the family out in force to deliberately annoy me?

"You never ans'red m'question las' night, Walker. Where be m'daughter, eh?" He smelled strongly of alcohol, although it wasn't much past ten-thirty.

"I have no idea where Colette is Mr Haywood, but I do know where your pigs were: destroying my parents' garden. We will be taking legal action if you fail to mend those fences of yours."

"Don' you go accusin' me, boy. Them fences be par' o' tha lane, an' tha lane bain't mine, she b'long t'yer pa an' 'im down Lower Valley Voo. Them fences were in good fettle las' time I looked, an' them hogs were in they field this mornin'!"

Then Chloë appeared, all simpering smiles and blinking eyes behind the layers of Dusty Springfield mascara.

"Pa, I've already told you. The field gate must have swung open – the catch is loose. You were supposed to have fixed it."

Laurie added, curtly, "I suspect the last time you checked *your* fences, Haywood, was months ago, and your hogs were in their field because *we* shooed them out from our garden into where they belong. Now, if you'll excuse me, I have a train to meet."

Just as curtly, he nodded to Chloë, took hold of my hand and marched out of the market. I could tell he was angry by the set of his jaw and length of his stride. I had to jog to keep up with him. I had heels on. It wasn't easy.

"Slow down!" I panted as I almost slipped over.

He stopped dead and I cannoned into him. "That man makes me wild," Laurie complained. "He's convinced that I took that wretched girl to London with me. I didn't. I wish I'd never asked her out now."

I wished he hadn't as well.

I glanced back into the market, I couldn't see Mr Haywood, but Chloë was standing to one side of the open doorway, hands on hips and scowling at us. She tossed her head and walked quickly away when she saw that I'd seen her. After childishly poking her tongue out at me.

"And what about Chloë?" I asked Laurie, resisting the urge to stick my tongue out back at her.

"What about her?"

"Nothing. I just wondered..."

"She's just a kid. She likes to think she's grown up and important, but she isn't."

I didn't agree with that assessment. The amount of makeup, and tight-fitting clothing that, even through winter-wear, clearly showed she did not bother with – nor needed – a bra, told all too well that she was perfectly aware of her adultness. I didn't say anything, though. Chloë was my age. Eighteen. Was I, then, also, 'just a kid' in his eyes?

He didn't notice my silence as we walked on up the hill to where we'd left the car behind the pens of the animal market. Most of the livestock, sheep, cattle and goats, had already been sold earlier in the morning – country folk start at the crack of dawn – so many pens were empty, apart from piles of dung and uneaten hay. Several men were starting to clear up with brooms, shovels and hoses.

Laurie stopped abruptly, turned to me, the cross expression leaving his face. "I'm sorry, love, I'm an ass. I didn't mean to mention Colette again."

It wasn't Colette who was bothering me, but I didn't want a row. "It doesn't matter." I stood on tiptoe to kiss his cheek. I felt quite daring doing so in public.

Laurie was a good bit taller than me, and he was standing uphill, so I had to stretch.

I didn't add, however, as I got into the car, his dad's Ford Escort, better than Laurie's battered old Morris Minor for picking his Gran up in, that I would rather *not* hear about Colette Haywood again.

Nor her sister, Chloë.

8

TRAIN OF THOUGHT

I believed that Laurie was joking when he casually mentioned that we had to request the train to stop at Umberleigh station. I was used to the London Underground where trains came every few minutes. You got on, squashed in like sardines in a can, especially if you'd timed it wrong and caught the rush hour, then pushed and shoved your way off again at the stop you wanted, your clothes and hair reeking of cigarette smoke, and very lucky if some greasy bloke hadn't fondled your bottom, or made a lewd comment about your 'assets'.

My familiar route was Walthamstow Central to Oxford Street where the large stores were located. I had plucked up courage to go to Carnaby Street once when I was fifteen, but I lost my nerve when the exotic cultures and rebellious identities of the people there made my shy modesty feel out of place. I was, I suppose, not really one for the Carnaby Army, or suited as a 'Dedicated Follower of Fashion' as in The Kinks' song. I went to the safe shops instead, the ones I knew from shopping with Aunt Madge – Selfridges, D.H. Evans and Saxone, the shoe shop where I bought a fabulous pair of black, pointed-toed shoes with kitten heels. Stupidly, I had worn them to school the next day, had promptly been given a detention and had to wear my gym plimsolls for the rest of the day – and to go home in, as I wasn't allowed to wear my lovely shoes with my school uniform. Which, incidentally, was hideous. Knee-length navy-blue pleated skirt, white blouse, two-tone blue tie, navy cardigan and a blazer. At least I had been able to do something about the skirt on the way to and from school – along with all the girls, I used to roll the waistband over several times to shorten its length. The ruse made our waists a bit bulky, but we pulled the blouse out to mask the effect.

Umberleigh was a rural station with a single line running from Exeter St David's to Barnstaple – although as we walked onto the platform, Laurie told me it went into a double line at Eggesford. "There's always a delay there, while the driver waits for the key."

I gave him a puzzled look. "Key? They need a key to start the train?"

He laughed and squeezed my hand, which was tucked firmly within his – although mainly because it was cold and I'd left my gloves in the car.

"It's more of a token than a key. There's only one, to indicate whether there's a train on the single track ahead – no token, means there is, so another train cannot proceed."

I nodded, understanding. That made sense, although I still did not believe Laurie about the station being a request stop. Buses, trams, yes. Trains, no.

I could see over to where there was building work going on – or rather, demolition. The station looked rather forlorn, not neglected but abandoned. When I remarked on this, Laurie explained that, until recently, the station master, Mr Simmons, and his family had lived in the house that adjoined the platform, and that the demolition work was the removal of the stock pens and buildings where animals had been kept prior to transportation.

"Apart from the builders, there's no one living or working here now." He added, somewhat forlornly. "Since Doctor Beeching advised Parliament to axe so many railway lines, the heart has gone out of many a rural community. Umberleigh was a hive of farming and agricultural industry; now it's just a platform where trains stop to let passengers on or off." He sighed and squeezed my hand. "But that's progress, I suppose. Although, I must say, I don't think much of it. Oh, look, there's Mrs Simmons!"

His morose mood brightened as a woman came onto the platform from the house, an old pair of gardening gloves and secateurs in her hand. She waved as she came towards us.

"Well, if it isn't Laurie Walker! Down from London for Christmas, be you?" She grinned, "I'd wager you be here to meet your gran?"

"I certainly am. This is Jan, my girlfriend – Jan, meet Mrs Simmons. the station master's wife."

The woman shook my hand. "Ex-station master. We've been relocated to Barnstaple. One of the lucky families. A lot of men have lost their jobs. I remember Laurie, here, for the times I told him off about his bike – he would just dump it anywhere, rather than put it in the shed. I threatened to toss it in the River Taw once, if I recall."

Laurie laughed and explained to me. "I was at college. I'd bike here from home and catch the train by the skin of my teeth, so I'd often just leap off the bike and run!"

"No being late for your grandmother, though!" Mrs Simmons laughed as she headed towards the nearest flower bed. "I'm doing a last tidy up before we have to entirely leave the place to its own devices." She breathed a little sigh that had a lot of obvious sadness behind it.

"Mrs Simmons has won the best kept station award several times," Laurie said. "Her flowers are always lovely; daffodils, roses and dahlias, depending on the season, of course."

I looked along the empty platform at the several raised flower beds. I could imagine the colours, a welcome sight to homecoming travellers or visiting arrivals. "Well," I announced with firm conviction, "even in its winter hibernation, I can tell this was all beautifully kept."

Mrs Simmons winked at Laurie and chuckled. "Take my advice, boy; this maid's a keeper!" She paused, cocked her head slightly to look down the line. "Train's coming."

I wondered how she knew. I hadn't noticed any signals or lights changing.

Laurie laughed and pointed to the metal tracks. "Listen carefully; you can hear them humming."

"What? Like cowboys do in westerns when they lie down and put their ear to the line?"

"Exactly, although I wouldn't recommend lying down here, or now." He pointed to the bend a few yards away as the engine appeared, and stepped to the edge of the platform. He held out his arm, although the train had already started to slow, so I still didn't know if he was having me on or not about requesting it to stop.

Two passengers, a young couple complete with walking boots and grey canvas rucksacks, emerged from the nearest carriage and headed for the road, and, I assumed, a footpath. Further along the platform, at the rear of the last carriage, a gentleman dressed in a black overcoat and wearing a black trilby hat, was assisting an elderly woman to alight by taking her suitcase, then offering his hand. Which she ignored.

Laurie's expression creased into a frown. "Wait here," he said gruffly as he marched off along the platform. Reaching the woman, he leaned forward to kiss her proffered cheek. This was Gran, then. I'd no idea who the chap was.

As the train began to pull away, I stood on my own, feeling like a lemon with its pith half scraped off, then a blast of ice-cold wind kicked me in the face, and one of my Aunt Madge's sayings sprang to mind: "Blow this for a game of conkers!" I mumbled and marched along the platform, setting a smile to my cold visage as the woman noticed me approaching and looked directly at me. Actually, she didn't look so elderly as I got closer. She wore a hint of make-up – a pale grey eyeshadow, a touch of mascara and red lipstick. Grey hair, neatly styled beneath a red felt hat with a pheasant feather poking out from a ribbon around the base of the crown. Sensible brogues, tweed suit, and she held an ebony, silver-topped walking cane which she raised slightly to point towards me.

"Is this your young lady?" The woman looked me up and down as if assessing me for a job interview, or I suppose, whether I appeared suitable as a prospective partner for her only grandson. I summoned the courage to return her scrutiny.

"Yes, Gran, this is Jan," Laurie said, and added to the gentleman, "I'll take the suitcase, sir."

"Jan? A shortened nickname?" Laurie's grandmother queried as I held out my hand to her. She nodded, but didn't return the handshake.

The gentleman, who looked quite stern with thin, colourless lips and disapproving lead-grey eyes, butted in, "Christian names are bestowed before God at the time of baptism, and should not be taken in vain by careless modification."

Gran – Mrs Brigham – ignored him, as did I. "Jan?" she asked me, "shortened from what? Janet? Janice?"

I was often asked this question. I only used my full name for official reasons, and, even then, if I could avoid 'January', I did. So, I was well practiced by dodging the question with a general answer.

I smiled and proffered my hand again. "Just Jan. I'm delighted to meet you, Mrs Brigham. Laurie's told me all about you."

This time she returned a brief, but firm, handshake, but said, "Lawrence, we do not use 'Laurie'. I expect he has told you that I am an interfering dragon who likes everything to be kept ship-shape and Bristol fashion? That I am set in my ways, and I do not suffer fools?"

They were his exact words, but to be tactful, I answered, "Not at all, he said how much he was looking forward to your visit."

"Tosh. Nor do I take to idle flattery, young lady. Reverend, thank you for your assistance, although I am not so infirm that I cannot carry my own luggage. You may be on your way."

Reverend? I realised, now, why he was dressed in black. I'd been concentrating on Mrs Brigham and hadn't noticed that he wore a vicar's dog-collar. Although, in my defence, he also wore a woolly scarf around his neck – home knitted, by the look of it, black, with a random pattern of little white crucifixes. It was the sort of item that doting aunts made for favourite nephews – or besotted ladies of the parish proffered with simpering giggles for birthdays or Christmas, so the recipient was obliged to wear the ghastly thing before managing to conveniently lose it.

He ignored Mrs Brigham and me, spoke to Laurie in a somewhat pompous but obsequious manner: "Give my regards to your mater and pater, Lawrence. Will we see you all for midnight mass on Christmas Eve?"

"It's DS Walker now, and no, I doubt it, Mr Passwith. We usually attend the Christmas morning carol service in Chittlehampton."

Mrs Brigham emitted a mild snort and mumbled, "You won't catch me in *any* church until various bishops start to do something about the general lack of adequate heating."

The reverend smiled condescendingly at her. "God's love keeps us warm, my dear lady." He turned to Laurie. "I am still referred to as 'reverend' not Mr. And you are now a detective sergeant? You have done well for yourself then, although reaching these ranks in the police force is fairly straightforward nowadays, so I hear."

"Not as straightforward as being able to recite a psalm, mutter a few prayers and turn up for work once a week on Sundays," Mrs Brigham stated, quite unabashed at her outright rudeness towards a man of the cloth.

Where had I heard the name Passwith? Then the penny dropped with a clang. "Oh," I said, "apple scrumping! You're the vicar who used to box Laurie's ears. I thought you'd retired?"

"Indeed, I tried my best to instil into the younger generations the meaning of morality, and yes, I have retired from active preaching, but once a vicar, always a vicar."

"Once a busybody, always a busybody," Mrs Brigham muttered.

I couldn't resist a laugh as I tucked my arm through Laurie's, "Once a policeman, always a policeman! But please, no one tell me that I am always going to be a library assistant!"

Laurie stroked his thumb over the back of my hand,

but said nothing. The other two did not even flicker a smile at my attempt at a joke.

Mrs Brigham pointed towards her luggage that had been set down on the platform and started to walk off. "Lawrence, bring my suitcase, please. I do not wish to linger. I hope your mother has the kettle on, and a better brand of tea than the one she purchased last time I visited. The stuff they served on the train from London was like dishwater. First Class is not what it used to be."

Laurie let go of my arm, hefted her suitcase to his shoulder and followed in her wake as if he were a Tibetan Sherpa.

I did not want to be rude, so I flashed the reverend a brief smile, told him that I was pleased to have met him (a lie) and scurried after my boyfriend and his grandmother, uncertain whether she was a formidable dragon or a secret pussycat.

Mrs Simmons, I noticed, had taken herself off to the far end of the platform and had her back to us. I wondered whether she was deliberately avoiding Grandma Brigham or the vicar. Or both?

"Have you a clean handkerchief in your pocket?" Mrs Brigham asked her grandson as we walked.

"Yes, Gran. Do you want to use it?"

"Certainly not! You need it to remove the smear of red lipstick from your mouth. I've no idea who has been so intimate, my boy, but I notice that your girlfriend wears a more refined shade of pink."

9

DRAGON'S BREATH

Dragon was, maybe, a little too harsh, but Gran Brigham was not – never would be – anything like a purring pussycat. Self-opinionated old bat would possibly be more appropriate, and, as we entered the house, I realised that Alf's jokes about hanging up the garlic, and the broomstick parked outside, held an element of understanding.

"No one has got around to repainting this front door, then," she remarked as we entered the house. Inside, as she removed her coat and handed it to me to hang up, she glanced at the grandfather clock. "As usual, ten minutes fast. Take my suitcase upstairs to my room, Lawrence, but do not put it on the bed. You never know what has brushed against luggage in transit. I have no desire to have muck on my bed covers. Ah, Elsie, you've put on weight, I see."

I felt so sorry for Laurie's mum as she came into the hall from the kitchen, wiping her wet hands on a towel. She had emerged with a smile on her face, which was instantly wiped away.

"Hello, Mummy. Was the journey ghastly?"

"It was. I don't know why I come all the way down

here." Mrs Brigham proffered a cheek for her daughter to dutifully kiss.

Laurie was half way up the stairs as Alf entered from the kitchen, his feet in socks only, having come into the house via the scullery and the back door, leaving his wellies behind and not stopping to put his slippers on.

"Hello, Ethel, I thought that must be your cauldron on the front doorstep. Laurie? Dump that case then come out to the garden; I need you."

"Alfred. I was just remarking on the unpainted front door and the fact that the clock is still not set right."

"Ah well, we can't go changing things and disappointing you, can we, Ethel? And it's Alf. I prefer Alf."

Mrs Walker looked stricken, but I managed to stifle a laugh when I caught Laurie's grin as he winked at me, then ran up the stairs to deposit his grandmother's case in her room. On the floor, I assumed, although I wouldn't have been surprised had he defied orders and put it on the bed.

"Shall I pour your tea, pet?" Elsie pleaded with her husband, obviously hoping for moral support, but Alf was already heading back into the kitchen, calling over his shoulder, "Not yet. There's something I need to show Laurie."

So it was just us three ladies who sat in the front room nursing best bone china cups and munching a light lunch of ham sandwiches, neatly cut into crust-less triangles. Bess, I noticed, had sensibly made a cursory sniff at Grandma Brigham then taken herself off to her basket beside the fire. Dogs know when they are not appreciated.

"So, Jan, you are a librarian?" Gran queried.

"I'm only a library assistant. You need qualifications to become a librarian."

"And you do not possess such qualifications?"

I nearly answered *no, not yet,* but why should I lie? I had no intention of doing an involved course in order to stay in a library for the rest of my life. I was quite happy being an ordinary assistant without any of the hassle of responsibilities – and with the freedom of pursuing my dream of becoming a published author. (OK, so there was more chance of Him Next Door's pigs flying, but what was wrong with ambition?) So, instead, I answered with a half truth: "I'm not sure if librarianship is the vocation I wish to follow. I might want to explore new challenges in a year or two."

To my surprise, she didn't come back with a scathing retort. She held out her cup for Elsie to refill and stated, "Do not put yourself down, girl, by saying 'only'. *Only* a library assistant? There are often far too many admirals and not enough sailors, and it's the sailors who keep the ship afloat. Where would we be without the workers? Bus drivers, shop assistants, waitresses, waiters – library assistants?"

I couldn't resist my answer. "We'd have not a single book shelved or overdue ticket written?"

She smiled. "Precisely. Admirals do not tend to dirty their hands with the," she paused, raised her refilled tea cup in a form of salute, "with stoking the boiler." She took a sip of her tea, grimaced. "Elsie, are you incapable of making a *hot* pot of tea? This is stone cold."

Flustered, Laurie's mother hurried to her feet, and sent her own cup and saucer flying. Fortunately, the cup was almost empty, but it smashed into pieces against the hefty stone of the chimney breast. I leapt up to help pick up the pieces. Grandma Brigham merely tutted and announced that she was going upstairs to unpack her case.

I really couldn't make her out. One moment she seemed relatively pleasant, the next, a Victorian matron akin to the queen's famous 'We are not amused!' façade.

Elsie, to give her *her* due, said nothing, but then, I expected that she was used to her mother's sharp tongue.

I ran to the kitchen to fetch a cloth to mop up the tea spill from the rug and almost collided with Laurie coming through the door from the opposite direction. He looked grim.

I knew that look. I'd seen it on my uncle's face often enough. "Is everything all right?" I asked, guessing that it wasn't.

He shook his head and went to the telephone in the hall. "Explain in a minute," he said as he dialled.

I found a dustpan and brush under the kitchen sink, and a cloth which I damped under the cold tap, and took the items into Elsie, then returned to the hall. A moment later she stood beside me, dustpan and broken china in hand, listening to Laurie speaking, standing, as I was, open mouthed in disbelief.

"Yes," he was saying into the telephone, "bones. Parts of a human skeleton, a decapitated skull, shoulder blades, pelvis, other bone fragments, and a pig's head." He paused, listening. "What? Yes, a *pig's* head – I bloody know what a pig's head looks like!"

He listened again, trying to contain his angry frustration. "The human, from the shape of the skull, is possibly female... No, of course I haven't bloody touched anything! What? What's that? Look I don't care how short staffed you are, get a SOCO team up here. We have a murder scene." Another short pause. "Well, it'll hardly be a kosher death, will it, seeing as how what's left of her has been buried in our compost heap! And no, I don't know why the pig is there, that's your job, not mine!" He slammed the phone down, then kicked the telephone table. "Ruddy imbeciles!" he muttered, "do they think I'm some kind of green behind the ears rookie?"

"Laurie, pet?" Elsie said, the broken china sliding to the floor from the dustpan as it tilted. "What is it?"

Laurie gazed at both of us for a moment, almost as if he hadn't realised that we were there. He shrugged, lifting his shoulders slowly, then letting them fall again. "Dad asked me to look at the well-rotted compost heap up the top end of the garden. Those pigs last night had rooted through it, made a right mess. He'd found an old sack, with," he ran his fingers through his short, brown hair, not wanting to say anything upsetting but he had no choice really. "With human remains in it."

Elsie put her free hand to her mouth, gave a little squeak of alarm. "What? Who is – was – it do you think?"

Laurie shrugged again. "No idea. I'd hazard a guess at one person assumed to be missing, but Colette Hayward only disappeared back in May, when I left for London. These remains are nothing but bare bone. A corpse would not have deteriorated that much in only a few months."

He stood staring at us both for a long moment, then queried his own question. "Would it?"

10

INTERLUDE: LAURIE

I'm a police officer, a Detective Sergeant, albeit a *very* newly promoted Detective Sergeant, although I had served my apprenticeship as a Detective Constable. Even so, despite what I'd said to Jan and Mum, I *was* green behind the ears in some areas. I mean, beyond the obvious skull, I hadn't seen that many unearthed partial skeletons to be able to accurately judge what I'd been looking at in Dad's compost heap. Nor, I confess, had I seen that many murdered dead bodies – fresh or old. I'd attended accidents, domestic and work place, where one or more unfortunates had died – a couple of the incidents had been quite gruesome. Traffic pile-ups are not for the faint-hearted, especially where children were concerned, but deliberate murder was not that common in North Devon, which was one reason why I had transferred up to The Smoke of London back in May – not because they had more murders, I hasten to add, but for the greater variety of cases to investigate.

I'd started off in Hackney, a rough, East End area, and I think I would have done well enough there, experience wise, if it hadn't been for the fact that my fellow colleagues were even rougher than the criminals we were supposed to be arresting. Corruption had been rife – if the rules could be bent or broken in favour of financial gain, then they were. I didn't believe in all that. If the law keepers do not keep the law, what hope is there for the law to be kept? I, therefore, took another transfer to what the Hackney people said was a back-of-beyond suburban nowhere.

To me, coming from the *real* back-of-beyond county of Devon, Chingford had seemed a thriving metropolis! My new Guv, DCI Toby Christopher, was a decent, honest copper who demanded – and got – respect. He also had Jan as his niece, so I doubly liked him, and hoped that he liked and trusted me enough in return, workwise *and* regarding my liking for Jan. I guess another confession needs to be aired here...

My first brutal murder scene had been in that same week I'd met Jan. Someone she knew from the library where she worked, an elderly lady. We'd discovered the body on walking back to my car after our first date. It had shaken me up a little. Death by accident or suicide, being in the wrong place at the wrong time, carelessness, or even sheer stupidity, was one thing, the deliberate cold cruelty of killing someone out of anger or hatred? That was something else. Don't get me wrong, as a constable I had attended 'unpleasant' scenes of crime, but I'd usually been the poor sod posted outside in the cold or pouring rain to keep the press and public away. It's one thing standing in uniform for hours trying to get as much shelter as you can, quite another being the one to find a battered corpse.

I wasn't totally certain what I was looking at with these human bones wrapped in a torn old piece of sacking, I elected to not peer too closely. DCI Christopher maintained that a crime scene should be left as uninterrupted as possible until a SOCO team –

scene of crime specialists, who took samples, fingerprints, photographs and such – arrived.

"Is that footprint from the murderer, or one of our own size-tens?" he'd say when reminding me to be careful. And, "Look first, take in the scene. What seems normal? What seems odd? What can you smell as well as see? Tobacco smoke, maybe? Did the victim smoke? If not, who did?"

Like I said, he was a good copper. If I was going to learn, I was fortunate to be learning from one of the best.

So, I told Dad not to touch anything; well, I yelled at him, for which I did hastily apologise, but he was about to remove the sack and its contents from where it lay in the compost heap. The area had already been disturbed enough by the pigs and our bumbling about chasing them last night. Although, it did run through my mind, was the sack there *before* last night? Had the sack of bones and the pig's head been dumped deliberately or as a joke, and the gate left open, allowing the pigs in? What came first, the chicken or the egg? In this case, the pigs or the bones?

Food scraps, garden waste, grass cuttings and such had been rotting down into good compost for well over a year, maybe even eighteen months. That sack could have been buried there for quite a while. Dad wouldn't have come across it until the heap was 'cooked' and ready for use.

What Dad *had* moved was the freshly slaughtered pig's head. He explained that he'd assumed it was a rather unpleasant joke or retribution from our neighbours, and, beyond moving it aside in disgust, had thought little of it. Then he'd found the partially buried sack with its gruesome contents.

The pigs, last night, had not chewed the pig's head. They would have eaten it had it been there.

Cannibalism is not taboo among pigs. Which meant it had been placed in our garden *after* we'd shooed those hogs out, but the human bones had been there before our porcine visitors had entered the garden. How could these be Colly's remains? I'd last seen her eight months ago. My knowledge of corpses might be hazy, but I knew perfectly well that a body buried in soil without a coffin, in our typical English climate, could take about eight *years* to become nothing more than bare bones. Assuming the corpse had been buried, of course. Left in a shallow grave, or no grave at all, decomposition could be quicker. Especially if animals had got at the corpse. And that seemed quite likely in this case, for, from my quick, cursory look, it seemed pretty obvious that something had gnawed at these remains. Teeth marks were quite prominent. The pigs last night? But, if they had chewed these bones, wouldn't they be scattered all around, not left inside the torn sack?

I had warned Dad, again, not to touch anything, and hurried to the house to call the local constabulary at Barnstaple station where I had worked prior to my relocation to London in May. All the while keeping my fingers crossed that someone competent would come out. DI Summers or DI Forbes would know their acorns. Or DS Fettle?

What I did not want was DS Frobisher to turn up. He was disinterested in anything that involved moving from behind his desk, or wasn't located inside a pub.

Needless to say, guess who I got.

11

TEA AND BONES

We stayed inside while the SOCO team did their work. Not that they did a lot. To be fair, there wasn't a lot they could do, the garden had been invaded by two pigs, Alf and Laurie had walked up and down when starting to tidy up – and Alf had been in and out of his greenhouse for days, weeks even – there was no telling how long that ghastly sack of remains had been there, buried in the matured compost heap waiting for two porkers to come and dig it up. Although, that would have happened soon after Christmas if the weather was clement enough, for Alf said several times, to anyone who had the patience to appear to be listening, that he had intended to spread the rich soil onto his raised veg beds in preparation for the coming of spring. I think it worried him that he could have found them any time. At least, now, Laurie was here to take charge of everything.

We sat in the front sitting room, drinking tea and nibbling at slices of rich and fruity home-made Christmas cake, quietly watching the team do what they had to do through the windows. We, being myself, Alf and Laurie. Elsie was exhausted – we'd been up for a good bit of the night, after all, and she was also somewhat shaken, so had taken herself upstairs for an afternoon lie down. I did rather wish that I could go up to my room as well, but Alf had poked the fire into life and stoked it with logs, so I curled up on one of the settees and dozed. Laurie tinkered at the piano for a little while, but his heart wasn't in it, so he closed the lid and went back to looking out of the window. I could tell that he was worried.

When the police had arrived, Gran Ethel had come down from her room to ascertain what all the fuss was about, had *harrumphed* when Laurie explained, made herself a small pot of tea and disappeared back upstairs with a tray and a chunk of cake in order to listen to *Afternoon Theatre* on Radio 4. A play by Alexander Pushkin called *The Queen of Spades*. Apparently, she listened to the radio, only she called it 'the wireless', every afternoon. Personally, I was a Radio 1 fan ever since Radio Caroline had been sunk – well, closed down and towed to Amsterdam as salvage in 1968. For the record, as nostalgic as the old pirate radio had been, Radio 1 broadcast far better reception, and in the spring before I left school in 1969, I'd collected several autographs of disc jockeys on the couple of occasions a friend and I had hung around outside London's Broadcasting House. You couldn't exactly do that with a ship wallowing at anchor somewhere in the North Sea, could you? I'd 'met' (if you could call 'Can I have your autograph, please?' as 'meeting'!) Johnny Walker, Noel Edmunds, Tony Blackburn, John Peel, Terry Wogan, Emperor Rosko ... I had all four of the Beatles' autographs as well. They had come to play at the Granada cinema, Walthamstow (the town next to Chingford) on 24th May 1963 – I was ten years old and George Harrison had been the second love of my life. The first was my pony, Rosie –

now retired and getting fat in a field. Uncle Toby, as a policeman, had been drafted in to assist with security arrangements and such. He'd managed to get two tickets for Aunt Madge and me at 7s 6d each – a fortune! *And* he had got their autographs for me. George had put *To Jan, love George,* and two XX kisses. It was one of my greatest treasures. We didn't hear or see much of the concert, though; too many girls (and boys!) standing up and screaming all the way through. Aunt Madge and I couldn't hear properly for several days after.

———

DS Frobisher, Laurie's Barnstaple counterpart, was everything that Laurie was not: untidily dressed, reeking of cigarette smoke and more than a hint of alcohol. Add to that, he was slapdash, dismissive and blatantly rude. My uncle would have had him demoted back to beat constable within hours. Or even dismissed.

He had arrived two hours after Laurie had reported the find, which was acceptable as detectives were rarely on the scene of a crime before it had been made secure. The pathologist had already arrived to start his preliminary appraisal and immediate witnesses questioned. Only DS Frobisher seemed to be in no hurry to get on with his job. He came into the house, leered at me and ordered, "Put the kettle on, darlin', I'm gaspin' for a cuppa. Three sugars." Not a single please or thank you. Nor did I like his surreptitious pinch to my bottom as I walked past him.

Out of the corner of my eye, I saw Laurie bristle with annoyance, but I flashed him a quick smile and disappeared into the kitchen, with the intention of staying out of the way as much as possible. As I went through the door, I heard Frobisher say, "She's a bit of all right, Walker. Posh totty, eh? Pass her on to me when she gets bored with you."

I paused for a second just inside the kitchen, wondering if Laurie would hit him, but I heard no sound of a fist connecting with a nose. Probably just as well, I didn't want Laurie to be arrested for assaulting a police officer.

It was, therefore, a relief when Frobisher took himself off up the garden and left us in peace. (I did suggest to Laurie that I assumed the initials DS stood for Disgusting Snot. That made him laugh.)

We watched as the pathologist left with the sack of bones and the pig's head, the SOCO team finished taking their samples of the soil, and inwardly groaned as Frobisher sauntered back to the house. At Laurie's suggestion, I made myself scarce in the kitchen with Bess for company.

Slightly raised voices wafted into the kitchen, coming from both Laurie and Alf, then the front door slammed and I heard Alf go upstairs. Laurie came into the kitchen, putting his outdoor coat on.

"Dad and I have to go to the police station, love. They want our statements, fingerprints and such."

"What? Now?" I squeaked, glancing outside at the onset of dusk. "Can't it wait until tomorrow?"

"Not really," he said with a sigh, "it's Christmas Eve tomorrow. Best to get it done and done with."

Alf popped his head around the door. "You ready, son? They want us to go with them in their Noddy car."

"I bet they won't want to give us a lift back, though," Laurie muttered.

"I'll telephone home when we're done. Mum can come and fetch us."

Laurie kissed me again, patted Bess, and the two of them were gone. I watched out of the window as the panda car's headlights swept up the dark lane then disappeared behind the high hedges and the bare-branched trees.

An ominous feeling, as heavy as the settling night, lodged itself in my stomach.

I knew enough of police procedure to know that a friendly request to go to a police station did not usually involve being 'invited' to use police transport.

That sort of 'courtesy' was usually confined to those under arrest.

12

HENS AND OWLS

It was dark by four-thirty, although the sky was lighter where the rising full moon was obscured by trees, hedges and the rounded hills. A cruel north-easterly wind had scuttled in, rattling, every so often, at the windows and squinnying in under the French doors, which led out to a paved area and the garden beyond. Elsie stoked the fire in the sitting room with applewood and ash logs and closed the thick blue velvet curtains designed to keep out draughts. At the last window, she stood a while, peering out at the strengthening dark. "We could be in for snow soon," she said, part worried, part wistful.

Gran Ethel immediately disagreed. "Too cold," she announced. "It'll not snow."

I saw Elsie bite her lip to keep a contradictory retort to herself and smiled at her. Had Laurie been here, we might have laid a bet on the matter; five new pence stake each. Snow? Or no snow?

I couldn't resist saying something. "Laurie said you often miss the bad weather here in this part of the valley. He said thunderstorms tend to go around the ridge, rather than over it?"

"Yes, that's right, pet. There's snow up on the Moor already, and often the village has a blanket, but they're on top of the ridge; we're tucked nicely away into this little hollow."

Gran tutted. "I do wish, Elsie, that you would stop using that vulgar term. *Pet*. Jan is not a dog or a cat."

"Oh, I don't mind, I like it," I answered – because I did.

"It was good enough for Grannie Jones," Elsie snapped back at her mother. "I use it because it reminds me of her." She closed the last two curtains, the curtain rings rattling along the wooden pole. "I have to shut the hens away. Come on, Bess." She clicked her fingers at the labrador, who bounded towards the hall, Elsie, head high, in her wake.

"Too sensitive by half, my daughter," Ethel tutted. "Always has been."

I changed the subject. "Shall I make a pot of tea?"

Just as I was pouring boiling water into the teapot, I heard Bess whining at the scullery door. I opened it to let her in.

"Ooh, you're freezing!" I exclaimed as she brushed against me. "Poor girl, you don't have nice warm hats, gloves and scarves like we do!" I laughed, "But then, you *do* have your own fur coat!"

I went back to pop the tea cosy on the pot. Where was Elsie?

"What have you done with your mistress, eh?" I asked Bess as I patted her head. "Left her out in the cold and dark all by herself, have you?"

Returning to the scullery I opened the back door and peered out into the night. The owl was hooting somewhere up the garden. It didn't sound as comforting as it had the night before.

"Elsie?" I called, "are you OK?"

Bess pushed past me and ran off up the garden in

the direction of the orchard, where the henhouse was – although I'd only glimpsed it from the path, I hadn't had time, yet, to fully explore.

"Elsie?" I called again.

The owl, disturbed by Bess, flew further off; hooted again. Unless the 'twit-twoo' had come from another owl?

I heard a different sound. A faint cry of some sort?

Bess came bounding back, whining.

There... again... Definitely a muted cry. I hesitated. Was Elsie, upset by her mother, taking a few solitary, secluded moments to herself?

"Elsie?" I called again, not too loud. "I've made tea."

Faint, almost a sob. "Help!"

I searched for a torch, found a small one in a basket by the back door, and completely forgetting that I only had slippers on, went out into the garden. Shining my feeble torch as best I could, I walked slowly up the path.

"Elsie?" I called several times, "Elsie?"

Then I saw her, crumpled half way up a flight of six, wide, stone steps. I ran.

"Elsie! Are you all right?" Stupid thing to say. Of course, she wasn't! She was half sitting, half lying, her knees drawn up, her left arm cradling her right. I trod on something that crunched. Elsie's torch. If it hadn't been broken before, it was now.

"I tripped," she muttered through chattering teeth – shock, cold and pain. Even with my faint torchlight, I could clearly see that her arm was broken and blood was trickling from a cut on her forehead. I could see something else, shining in the strengthening moonlight as well, but that small glimpse was gone as clouds whipped across the moon. I forgot about it. I had other things to think about.

I hauled off my fluffy woolly jumper and wrapped it around her shoulders. "Stay here," I ordered. (Another stupid thing to say, she was not going anywhere!) "I'll get help."

I lost a slipper running back to the house, wasted a few seconds finding it. Reached the house, tore inside.

"Ethel! Ethel! Elsie's had a fall – she's broken her arm!"

To give Gran her due, she didn't fuss. She calmly put on her coat, seeing me shivering, tossed me mine from the rack in the hall, shut Bess in the sitting room and told me to fetch blankets from the linen cupboard on the upstairs landing.

I took a quick moment to dash up to my room and change the slippers for shoes. She had already gone by the time I got downstairs again, although I could see the light from her torch bobbing along the path ahead. This one was large and bright, unlike the pathetic little thing I had. When I caught up, Ethel took the blankets from me and carefully wrapped them around her daughter.

"Run back to the house and call for an ambulance. Tell them we have had a fall, the ulna near the wrist looks fractured and there is a head injury. You know the address to send them to?"

I nodded.

"No," Elsie counter-commanded, wincing in pain. "The hens need shutting away or the fox will get them. And I don't want an ambulance."

"Don't be silly, of course you do."

"Alf will take me to casualty when he gets back."

"That's ridiculous. He could be hours at the police station."

"Never-the-less..." Elsie tried to get to her feet. Failed.

Gran tutted. "See to the hens, Jan, then we'll get her

up and into the car. I'll drive her to casualty at the infirmary."

"You can drive?" I said, a little too surprised. I guess it always seems odd when old people can drive a car. To be honest, though, Ethel must only have been about seventy. (OK. Old.)

Her response was indignant. "I can drive anything from one of those dinky car Mini-Minors to an army lorry, with a London omnibus or a farm tractor in between. I also have a basic knowledge of mechanics – and first aid. We had to be able to turn to anything during the war, you know."

I didn't know, nor did I know how to answer, so I hurried off up the garden, although I didn't know what I was supposed do with the chickens, either. When I got to the henhouse – a wooden garden shed, I shone my torch inside and was confronted by a dozen balls of red feathers bundled together in clean straw along a raised shelf, the ladies' little black eyes blinking at me in the torchlight.

"Oh, sorry, I didn't mean to wake you," I muttered, feeling a bit foolish for talking to hens. But I was answered – honest! Two of them gave me a little 'puk-puk' noise which sounded exactly like 'night-night'. Did I have to check for eggs or anything? I figured not, that seemed more like a morning task. I did look to see if they had water – they did, a metal bowl – so I shut the shed door and shot the bolt home.

When I got back to the steps, Gran had fashioned a makeshift sling using a headscarf, which I assumed had been in her coat pocket, and Elsie was insisting on getting to her feet, so, as gently as we could, we helped her up, and slowly, one on each side, step by painful step, got her back to the house. Gran found the keys to Laurie's Morris Minor on the key rack by the kitchen door, and although poor Elsie was in a lot of pain and feeling faint, we managed to get her into the car.

"Will you be all right on your own?" Gran asked me. I heard the tinge of doubt in her voice.

"Of course I will!" I lied.

13

A VISITOR

I was on the edge of panic. What to do? I was in a strange house. On my own. I stood in the hall by the telephone, listening to the only sound – the slow, measured, *tick...tock* of the grandfather clock. What to do? Aunt Madge would know!

Without thinking things through, I lifted the receiver and dialled home. The telephone at the other end rang. And rang, and rang, and rang. Gulping threatening tears of frustration, I put the receiver down. They were out. How dare Aunt Madge and Uncle Toby be out! I went to sit on the stairs. Why shouldn't they be out? It was the evening before Christmas Eve, after all. They were entitled to go to friends, or for a drink or – what did they do when they were on their own, I wondered?

Bess was at my side. She licked my hand, I rubbed her ears.

"Now look, Jan," I said aloud, sternly, to myself, "You're not a kid." That little insipid tick of malicious jealousy sparked in my mind again: *Despite what Laurie thinks.* I shoved it away. "You are not a kid. Pull yourself together!"

I wandered into the kitchen, put the kettle on. Bess looked hopefully at an empty bowl on the floor in one corner. I couldn't feed her as I had no idea what to give her. The kettle boiled, I lifted the teapot from the kitchen table and remembered that it was already full from the tea I had been making earlier. Stone cold now. I tipped it away, made myself a fresh brew. Bess, sitting beside me at the table, suddenly jumped up and ran into the hall, barking like the Hound of the Baskervilles. There came a knock at the front door.

I hesitated. Should I ignore it? The rat-tat-tat came again. I answered it.

I stood in the hallway, door wide open, staring blankly at a man dressed all in black, Bess wagging her tail at my side. Please, don't laugh: I seriously thought he was an undertaker come to tell me bad news.

I know. I'm an idiot.

"Good evening, Miss...? Er, my apologies, you were only introduced to me as Jan?"

I realised he was the Reverend Passwith, not the Grim Reaper.

"Jan Christopher," I answered, somewhat blandly. Despite the cold wind outside, his face was blotched and sweaty. He was a little out of breath, too. He lifted his hand and removed his hat. I caught a glimpse of the inside hatband. It was black-ringed with grime from his Brylcreemed hair. "Good evening, then, Miss Christopher. I'm delivering my Christmas cards. Is the Lady of the House at home?"

I've no idea why I lied, beyond I thought the man to be a creep. "She's lying down." Not so much of a lie. She probably was, or soon would be.

"I understand that the police were here earlier. Is everything all right?" He gave a sorry little chuckle. "No one murdered or anything?"

"We're all still very much alive," I answered,

smiling sweetly. There followed an awkward silence, during which I assumed he was hoping that I would invite him in.

A thought confirmed when he said, "I walked from the village. These hills are very steep in places, aren't they? And it is somewhat chilly. A cup of tea, perhaps?"

"A healthy walk is good for body and soul, don't you think? Oh! Hello!" I waved, putting on a bright expression to someone who had suddenly appeared at the garden gate. The small gate opposite the front door, which I'd been told was rarely used because the larger gate nearer the garage-barn, and where the post box for delivered mail was situated, was more practical.

Chloë Haywood's face was lit up by the outdoor security light above the porch that the reverend's appearance had activated. The sparrows in the honeysuckle were complaining. *Put that light out!*

"I've come t'see Laurie," Chloë said, opening the gate and stepping onto the path. With her other hand, she was tucking something into her pocket. "He said I could."

Did he, now? I thought. Said, somewhat acidly, "He isn't here."

The reverend had turned to see who had arrived. "Ah! Miss Haywood, just the person. Is your father at home?" He replaced his hat, nodded goodbye to me and strode towards the gate.

"Good, you can bother her, instead," I muttered as I made to close the front door.

There was a peculiar thing about this part of the valley (other parts as well, for all I knew) that I had already noticed: sound carried. Not as an echo, but the valley's acoustics were like a sort of megaphone or hands cupped around your mouth effect. I heard the garden gate click shut, and the reverend saying, "Did your father get to the market?"

On impulse, I switched off the hall light so there'd be no tell-tale streak showing, and opened the door a little wider to listen.

"What's it t'you if he did?" Chloë answered.

"He was supposed to get something for me. I'd given him money for the purchase."

Chloë laughed. It wasn't a pretty laugh, more of a mocking bray. "So that's where 'e got the dosh t'get sloshed. I wondered."

"Is he at home? They've had the police here today. Did you know?"

I couldn't hear the answer. The owl hooted, long and loud from the oak tree.

I was starting to go off owls.

14

A HUNGRY DOG AND A FLYING BEAR

Was it any surprise that I felt uneasy? I was alone, in a house I didn't know, with it being dark and unfamiliar outside. The nearest neighbour, a quarter-of-a-mile away, was an unfriendly, antisocial nightmare with a daughter to match, and the other neighbour, half-a-mile away further down the hill, unknown to me. The grandfather clock struck six. I slid the front door bolt home, then went to check that the scullery door was locked, checked the French doors in the sitting room, too. While I was there, I shoved a few more logs on the fire. The room was quiet, but warm and cosy, the Christmas lights on the tree twinkled prettily. So quiet. *Too* quiet. Apart from a rather loud grumble from my stomach.

Hungry, I wandered to the kitchen, found the biscuit tin and devoured four digestives. Should I think about preparing something to eat for dinner? Everyone would be hungry when they got back. If they got back. Elsie had said something about a casserole that she'd prepared earlier.

What if they kept her overnight at the Infirmary and Gran Ethel stayed with her? What if Barnstaple police arrested Alf and Laurie? Unlikely, surely? They'd only *found* those bones, Alf hadn't dumped them there, had he? That led to the question of who had. And whose bones were they?

Then even more urgent questions. When would Laurie be home with Alf? I didn't fancy cooking something just for myself – although there was also Bess. Poor Bess was looking mournfully at me, her brown eyes conveying that she was wasting away to skin and bone. I rather wished I hadn't been reminded of bones... Succumbing to her doggy telepathy, I found some tins of dog food in the scullery and opened one for her. PAL: *Prolongs Active Life.* A rather macabre thought entered my head. Whoever had been those bones, should have tried eating some dog food.

I wandered back into the cosy sitting room, my thoughts returning to Reverend Passwith as I passed through the hall. He'd said he was delivering a Christmas card. Well, he hadn't given me one. Perhaps he'd put it in the postbox. Should I go and look?

I peeped behind one of the drawn curtains, peering out into the night through the glass of the window. Maybe not. It would still be there in the morning. Something else caught my eye, a fluttered movement. Then another. Leaves falling? Goodness! It was snowing! I stood at the window watching as the few haphazard flakes grew more in number, swirling and dancing as the gusting wind huffed and puffed. None of the snowflakes seemed to be landing, just little whirlpools of flakes twisting around and around, then skittering sideways before twirling crazily again. It reminded me of a flock of starlings when they perform their intricate in-flight dances. A murmuration of starlings. A murmuration of snow? What if it snowed hard? What if I got snowed in, all on my own? I suppose I could always walk up to the village, ask for help?

The snow stopped. It had only been a flurry.

Why would you get hot, sweaty and out of breath if you walked *from* the village? You'd be going *down*hill, not up. What had Reverend Passwith wanted Godfrey Haywood to get for him? Why hadn't he called at their house, Upper Valley View first, as he'd passed by? Why had he come here? I didn't believe a word about the card business. Plain nosiness, perhaps? And what did Chloë Haywood want with Laurie? Had he *really* told her to call round? If so, why? And why hadn't he mentioned it to me?

I pulled the curtain closed, put another log on the fire and went upstairs to my bedroom. Thinking about unanswerable question after unanswerable question was silly. Find yourself something to do, Jan. Something positive!

I'd brought some wrapping paper, scissors and sticky tape from home, so amused myself for half-an-hour wrapping up and labelling the couple of little presents I'd bought from the market, including the photograph album. Laurie had hidden the hyacinths in a shed somewhere, out of his mum's sight. I flipped through the book I'd bought for myself then put it safely in my empty suitcase, along with a leftover piece of wrapping paper and the roll of sticky tape.

I looked at the writing pad next to my bed. I could jot down some ideas for the next chapter of the science-fiction novel I was writing. I'd left my hero, Radger (rhymes with Badger) Knight hiding from a unit of elite Starforce Five soldiers in an Albaldah tavern basement in the Sagittarius Sector. While hiding, he'd found a few kegs of highly valuable Venusian Vino. I had to help him figure out how he could a) steal them, b) smuggle them out of the star system, c) stay alive while doing so. Unfortunately, I was as stumped for ideas as he was. I sat for a while, pen in hand, gave up. I had no concentration for my masterpiece future bestselling novel.

"What are you looking at, Bear?" I grumbled at Teddy, giving him a mock punch to his nose, then swept him into my arms for a cuddle. Still clasping him, I wandered to the window. There had been a little more snow, a scatter of white on the hedges, trees and the edges of the path where the wind had blown it. The sky lit up and I saw the headlights of a car sweep past the house – I opened the window, leaned out... and promptly sent Bee Bear flying into the night air.

15

HEADLIGHTS

Leaning over the gate and peering along the lane, I could see that a white car had pulled up beside the barn-come-garage. I didn't want to walk up through the allotment part of the garden in case I stumbled across any more bones that hadn't been found – or the ghost of those that had – so I let myself out into the lane through the small gate and walked down the hill, Bess trotting ahead, her tail wagging. Stupidly, I should have put a coat on for there were a few more flurries of snow tossing about in the restless wind, although the hedges to either side were high, and provided some shelter. I could hear sheep bleating from somewhere ahead, and the sound of a tractor's engine. A farmer out feeding hay to his flock. At least the sheep had their thick fleeces to keep themselves warm. From somewhere nearby, a pheasant cackled his alarm call – pheasants were daft birds; they would run ahead of a car for ages rather than using their common sense and wings to fly away to safety over a hedge or fence.

"Hello?" I called as a lady emerged from the passenger side of the car. I shone my torch in her direction, but the beam wasn't strong enough to light up much beyond a yard or so ahead. "Can I help you? Are you looking for Mr or Mrs Walker?"

"Not really," came a laughing voice in reply, a voice I recognised. "You'll do nicely enough!"

I couldn't believe what I was hearing, seeing, as I ran forward into her outstretched arms.

"Aunt Madge! Aunt Madge!" I squealed, "what are you doing here?" I didn't give her chance to answer as I dashed round to the driver's side to hug Uncle Toby as he, chuckling, got out of the car.

"We arranged it weeks ago," Madge grinned, re-emerging from the car with her coat and handbag. "Laurie thought it would be fun to surprise you!"

"Who's this then?" my uncle asked, patting Bess on the head, "and can we get inside? It's a tad chilly out here."

I couldn't help it, relief swamped through me like a sudden tidal wave. Clinging tightly to him, I burst into tears.

"Hey, sweetheart, what's wrong?" he asked, concerned, lifting my chin with one finger and tipping my face upward to kiss me on the forehead.

"Alf's been arrested, Laurie's got another girlfriend, Elsie nearly broke her neck, Ethel can drive a bus, the reverend's like an undertaker, and I've lost Bee Bear!"

"I'm not sure if that's all terribly worrying or extraordinarily exciting," Aunt Madge observed drily, "but can we go indoors? I'm desperate for a tinkle!"

Uncle Toby rubbed my tears away with his thumb, "Come on, Cupcake, you can tell us all about it after Madge has ensured that she isn't going to flood everywhere below deck."

That made me laugh, as he knew it would.

I put the kettle on while Aunt Madge made use of the downstairs cloakroom, then we sat at the kitchen table warming our hands and insides with hot cups of tea; Uncle Toby surreptitiously feeding Bess bits of biscuit while I related all that had happened in a less dramatic, more coherent manner.

"There's not a lot we can do tonight," Uncle Toby said, pushing his chair back and getting to his feet when I had finished. "I'll fetch our luggage in, then take a drive up to the police station, see what's what."

"Is that a good idea?" Aunt Madge objected as she cleared the table of cups, saucers and biscuit crumbs. "They'll not want an outsider DCI poking his nose in, surely?"

"That they would not, but the Chief Superintendent and I go back a long way, it would be rude of me not to call in and suggest a Christmas drink, don't you think?"

Aunt Madge rested one hand on her hip in her 'scathing stance', as Uncle Toby called it. "As if he will be there this time at night, Toby!"

Her husband smiled and kissed her on the cheek. "Of course, he'll not be there, but I'm not to know that, am I?" He winked at me, then added, "Come on, Cupcake, help me with our suitcases, then we'd better put out an APB call for this absconded bear of yours before a farmer shoots him for chasing sheep."

"And while you two do that, Mrs Walker said something about having a chicken casserole ready for us all when I spoke to her on the telephone yesterday. I'd better rummage for it."

Uncle Toby and I left Aunt Madge happily 'rummaging' through the larder. She was a wonderful cook and even more wonderful at getting thing organised. I knew that, before long, the aga would be hot, the casserole would be warming, the sitting room fire stoked, the suitcases unpacked and everything sorted.

"There's only one empty bedroom upstairs," I said

as I put on my coat. "I did wonder, when I took a sneak peek this morning, why it looked so freshly aired, with towels laid out and flowers in a vase on the windowsill!"

I found Bee Bear, looking most disgruntled, sitting in the middle of the garden path. The owl was in a nearby tree – I could hear him, although not see him – and the full moon had risen high above the hedges. With the smattering of snow glistening, the fresh, crisp air and the quiet (apart from the owl) stillness, now that the tractor had gone and the sheep were fed, everything looked serene and lovely.

A rather damp and disgruntled Bee Bear, however, didn't seem to appreciate the tranquil scenery as much as I did.

16

INTERLUDE: LAURIE

I sighed and stretched my aching back and shoulders. The hard wooden chair was not exactly comfortable. How long was DS Frobisher intending to keep us at Barnstaple? I'd told him, at least four times, all I knew. I had dropped Colette Haywood off at the station, then driven home because I'd forgotten the packed lunch that mum had made for me – I had thought about not bothering, but she would have been upset as she always put little surprises in with the more mundane things of cheese and pickle sandwiches, bag of crisps and chunk of cherry cake. On this occasion, she'd added a chocolate bar and a crisp new £5 note tucked inside a 'good luck, we love you' card.

I rather wish I hadn't told him that bit, because he immediately jumped to the conclusion that I'd returned home to dump Colette's body in the compost heap.

"Why?" I asked him. "What possible motive could I have had?"

His answer stunned me. I hadn't known, had no inkling. Chloë had filled the police in with all the details when Colette had first gone missing back in the spring. Whether their father knew was conjecture on my part, as Frobisher didn't elucidate.

Colette had been pregnant when she had disappeared. Three months. A time period to put me in the frame for being the father, and, according to Detective Sergeant bloody Frobisher, giving me a perfect motive to do away with her.

It didn't matter that I denied any possibility because I'd only gone to the pictures and the pub with the girl – no 'relations' had taken place. (*My* word, Frobisher used something far more crude that began with an 'f'.) Nor would he listen to me when I told him that I knew she was no stranger to other men. I wouldn't say she was a tart, to use common parlance, but nor was she pure and innocent. There was the ex-boyfriend we'd arrested for assault and burglary, for a start!

Beside which, did Frobisher know who those bones were? They had been picked clean, and didn't look 'new' to me, although I'd be the first to admit I was no forensic pathologist. As far as I was concerned – and I told Frobisher so – two other local women were unaccounted for. Mrs Haywood and the Reverend Passwith's wife.

Frobisher openly scoffed.

"Haywood's wife went off with her fancy-man, that's common knowledge, and are you seriously suggesting that a man of the cloth done in his Missus and left her to rot in your pa's rubbish heap?"

"Common knowledge is not factual evidence," I answered, with an edge of irritation, "and ordination as a priest does not automatically carry a passport to sainthood. Those remains could not have been in my father's compost heap for long."

He turned his compost heaps over every couple of months, although he'd admitted to me that he couldn't remember when he'd last done it. But it had been turned at least once since I left in May.

We hadn't mentioned the pig's head.

"Oh, so you're an expert on human remains now, are you? Learnt about them from your fancy London friends, did you?"

It was only the fact that I would be in serious trouble that kept me from hitting him.

I was left alone in the interview room for a good while. Could have murdered a cup of tea and a bite to eat, but I knew that the canteen would be shut, and, even if it wasn't, Frobisher would rather see me starve than offer even a stale crust.

Raised voices filtered into the room. I ignored them. A drunk squabbling with the duty sergeant? So, I was surprised when the door opened, and a grump-faced surly Frobisher told me I could go. I sat staring at him for a good half-minute.

Frobisher opened the door wider. "You're in the clear, for now, but don't go disappearing. We'll have further questions when forensics come through."

I said nothing as I walked past him and headed for the Way Out. I was relieved to see Dad putting his coat on, but more than a dozen questions rammed into my head when I saw DCI Christopher standing behind him.

"I leave you alone for five minutes," my boss said with a grimace, "and you manage to get yourself straight into a pile of whatsit."

"My compost heap," Dad protested, indignantly, "is quality organic fertilizer, I'll have you know."

"Complete with bonemeal," I added.

Gallows humour.

An unfortunate trait of many a copper.

17

WELL I NEVER!

Uncle Toby and Laurie came straight back from the police station, after dropping Alf off at the infirmary and a quick check on how Elsie was doing. I was anxious to see Laurie – I suspected that I had as many questions as the Devon and Cornwall Police to ask him, but my own interrogation was swept aside as he walked wearily into the kitchen beside my uncle. He looked as white as a ghost and as tired as an insomniac.

I had started to ask a question but Uncle Toby raised a stern finger. "No questions until we've eaten."

A fair enough, reasonable order, so I helped Aunt Madge dish up casserole for the four of us which we wolfed down with chunks of buttered bread – not bothering with the dining room, content with the kitchen table.

We'd just finished eating when Bess started barking and Alf and Gran arrived home. Laurie and I hurried into the hall. They both looked shattered.

"We've a casserole keeping warm in the oven," I said, pointing towards the kitchen, "I expect you're famished? Is Elsie all right?"

"Settled into a ward; keeping her in for the night.

Worried about the gash to her head and possible concussion more than the break to her arm." Alf said, sniffing the air. "Oh, that food smells good; let me have a quick visit to the bathroom and I'll be with you."

"Come on, Gran," Laurie said, taking his gran's coat and offering her his arm.

"Are we not eating in the dining room?" she asked with a disapproving raised eyebrow.

Laurie answered diplomatically. "The kitchen is warm, friendly and less bother. Come and meet Jan's folks. They're nice people."

Uncle Toby must have heard for he was laughing as we went into the kitchen. "You say things like that to your superiors on a regular basis, lad, you'll soon make superintendent." He was walking towards the door, hand outstretched. "Good evening, Mrs Brigham, I'm..." But he stopped dead, as if one of the aliens in my science fiction tales had zapped him with a stun gun.

Gran Ethel was standing stock still as well.

They both spoke at once; "Well I never!"... "Goodness me!"

Uncle Toby recovered first. "Miss Jones! It must be all of twenty-six years?"

Gran actually smiled. "I believe you left us in August 1945, and I was, technically, Mrs Brigham back then, but I had continued to use my maiden name throughout the war. Jones was more unidentifiable. I tried to convince you to remain with us, as I recall."

"*Mmm hmmm*? The war was over, and I wanted to become a detective constable – and husband to my good lady, here."

Gran Ethel regarded Aunt Madge, then held out her hand. "Yes, I remember you, Miss Marjorie Bolton-Chalmers. You were one of Churchill's secretaries, I believe?"

Aunt Madge nodded. Laurie and I stood just inside the doorway, open-mouthed, both of us having lost the gist of the conversation with no idea what they were talking about. Alf came in and looked as bewildered as we did.

Inviting us all to sit at the table, Aunt Madge came to our rescue as she started to dish up the casserole for Gran and Alf – with seconds for the rest of us.

"Toby worked with your grandmother, Laurie, as, well... doing something for the war effort at a place called Bletchley Park. My parents lived very nearby and I knew several of the ATS and WRENs who also worked there. I met Toby one evening when I was home for the weekend."

"Miss Jones – Mrs Brigham – was my boss there," Toby added with an amused smile. "I never even considered that she was your grandmother, Laurie."

"And you worked for Winston Churchill, Aunt Madge?" I asked, awed. She had never said a word about it before.

"We are not really allowed to speak of those days, dear," she said, setting down her own plate and joining us at the table. "A lot of what many of us did is hush hush. Maybe one day the secrecy will be lifted."

I noticed Gran nod, her lips set in a firm line. "I hope you remember that rule, Tobias Christopher?"

"Of course," he replied, "though I prefer *Toby* just as much now as I did then, not Tobias."

Gran snorted. "And I do not hold with shortening names any more now than I did then."

"Churchill was always shortening things," Madge said blowing on a forkful of hot chicken before popping it into her mouth. "He signed many of his letters K.B.O. I assumed it was some sort of secret code. It took me weeks to find out what it was short for." She ate another mouthful. Laurie, Alf and I stared at her.

"Well?" I finally burst out, "what was it!"

Gran answered for my aunt. "We all got them. It was his way of giving everyone a sort of pep talk: Keep Buggering On."

We laughed.

"So," I said with a tentative laugh, "I assume that despite the best efforts of Barnstaple Police to arrest the wrong people, and the concern of the North Devon Infirmary, we KBO?"

I then sat, patiently waiting for Aunt Madge to pour coffee for us all, but as the sugar bowl was passed round, I gave in to impatience. "Do we know anything about those awful remains?" I asked.

Laurie shook his head. "They told Dad and me next to nothing, apart from accusing me of murdering Colette then disposing of her."

"Which is pretty much conjecture at best, circumstantial at worst," Uncle Toby added. "There will be no information until the pathologist makes his report, and forensics come back with anything relevant."

"They might not have been in my compost heap for long, maybe a couple of months, maybe only a few days," Alf said, "The pig's head, however, could only have been there a few hours."

"Deliberately planted, then?" Aunt Madge suggested.

"Someone trying to put blame on you. Drawing attention to bones that hadn't been found?" Gran Ethel offered a different option. "A bit of a coincidence the day you return home, don't you think? And we all know the derogatory term – a pig meaning the police."

"I thought that as well," Laurie nodded.

I told them about the Reverend Passwith calling at the house, and how he had hurried off with Chloë.

"Again, probably not connected with our situation. Coincidence and conjecture," my uncle pointed out.

"But it is not coincidence, nor conjecture, that someone deliberately wanted to injure Elsie," Gran said as she dabbed her mouth with a napkin, her plate now empty.

We all looked at her. She calmly sipped at the coffee Aunt Madge had poured for her.

"My daughter, for she is always such a nuisance leaving everything to the last minute – should have shut those hens away before it grew dark – did not fall by accident. There was wire stretched across the steps."

18

CHRISTMAS EVE – BREAKFAST

Too dark, too cold, and all of us too tired, we left investigating Gran's revelation about the wire until morning. We all slept like logs, even Alf, despite his worrying about his wife, because when we gathered for breakfast, he said he'd gone out like a light as soon as his head had hit the pillow.

Aunt Madge conjured up breakfast, served in style in the dining room given that it was Christmas Eve and therefore special. She had set everything out as if we were in that grand Belgravia London house in the new Edwardian TV drama *Upstairs, Downstairs*. China tureens of sausages, bacon, scrambled eggs and mushrooms on the sideboard for us to help ourselves to whatever we wanted to eat. Racks of toast, butter pats in beautiful little dishes. Tea, coffee, fruit juice. All that was missing were the main characters from 'Downstairs' – Hudson the butler and head maid, Rose. Aunt Madge is marvellous at organising this sort of thing – though she must have got up at the crack of dawn to find and prepare everything.

Gran had the grace to be appreciative, although her

"This is nice," was utterly spoilt when she'd added, "so much more civilised than eating in a kitchen.'

Uncle Toby evened things out, however, with, "But a warm farmhouse kitchen beats those horrendous canteen barracks that always smelled of over-cooked cabbage and disinfectant, don't you think?"

Breakfast done and cleared, we donned coats and outdoor shoes and trooped into the garden. There had been another light dusting of snow overnight, but the morning was bright and crisp. Blue sky, fluffy clouds.

Laurie had beaten us all to it much earlier when he went to let the hens out.

"Just here," he said pointing to the fairly solid trunk of a Winter Jasmine bush that was covered in little yellow, snow-flecked flowers. There was a distinctive groove visible where wire had cut in, and on the opposite side of the steps, (a vigorous Camelia) a remnant of wire was still twisted around the lower stem of the shrub.

"Someone must have come back to remove the wire," he said. "I've looked all round; if Mum had merely broken it, both ends would still be trailing."

I immediately thought of Chloë tucking something into her pocket. "Can anyone get into the garden from further up the lane?" I asked, "I mean, from behind the henhouse, or something?"

"Yes," Laurie answered, "there's a small gate in the top boundary hedge. You'd have to climb over, though; we keep it padlocked."

"There's a footprint here," Uncle Toby said, pointing to the soil beneath the plant. "Wellington boot. Size six or seven?"

"Could as easily have been Mum's," Laurie said.

"*Mmm hmmm*, possibly. Where's this compost heap, then?" Uncle Toby asked. Laurie led the way.

It wasn't much to inspect. The police had dug it over, Alf said he wished they'd done more of the garden while they were at it, but there was nothing for us to see except rich, dark soil and a few annoyed woodlice. What sort of clues could be left in a winter garden anyway? Especially after two pigs had made such a mess.

"Beyond waiting for forensics and any identification, there's nothing we can do," observed Uncle Toby. He shrugged, "And even then, it's not our case, so, well, I wouldn't mind a coffee?"

We all agreed that was a good idea, but as we were wandering back to the house, Aunt Madge (who'd insisted on playing the 'downstairs' role of doing the washing up) called from the front door.

"Toby? Toby! Telephone for you!"

My uncle frowned. "Now, who could be calling me down here? It had better not be a summons to return to Chingford for some reason or other. I'm on long overdue leave!"

"We never had such a thing as 'leave' during the war," Gran said with an audible sniff. "Our work was too important."

Uncle Toby laughed, "You mean, *you* never took any leave. I had some very enjoyable weekends off."

"With Aunt Madge?" I asked.

He didn't actually answer, all I got was a broad smile and his customary *mmm hmm,* which could cover a multitude of meanings from amicable agreement to discreet 'mind-your-own-business'.

We dumped our coats and boots in the scullery and assembled round the kitchen table for coffee. Gran had tea but didn't seem to object to a nice warm kitchen this time. The door to the hall was open, so we could hear Uncle Toby's conversation, only it was more of a one-sided monologue consisting of words such as, "Well, yes, but..." and, "I see, but..." There were quite a few 'buts'.

We heard him say "Oh, very well, goodbye," and a slight clatter as he put the receiver down – then immediately the telephone rang again. More of "I see" and a "Thank you, yes, I'll tell him. Yes."

He was smiling as he walked into the kitchen and gratefully took the black coffee Aunt Madge offered him.

"Elsie is ready to come home," he announced as he sat down. "That was the hospital, I agreed that you would collect her straight away, Alf,"

Alf beamed and finished his coffee in one gulp. "I'll get the car."

His grin faded as Gran said, "I'll come with you."

"Actually," Uncle Toby contradicted her, "I'd be rather grateful if you stayed here. There's a couple of things I'd like to mull over, and your 'little grey cells', to quote Hercule Poirot, might come in handy?"

Alf beamed again, collected his car keys and, scared his mother-in-law might change her mind, left as quickly as if he were chasing to put out a fire.

We refilled our coffee cups (another tea for Gran) and waited expectantly for Uncle Toby to begin what held the distinct air of a pow-wow.

19

PLANS OF ACTION

"That was Barnstaple's Chief Superintendent Moorcroft on the 'phone," Uncle Toby began, somewhat grimly. "He regrets he cannot take me up on the message I left him yesterday evening, of an offer to meet for a Christmas drink somewhere..."

"Thank goodness for that!" Aunt Madge interjected, "I have enough of policemen's talk back at home."

"You might not have been invited to join us!" my uncle quipped.

Aunt Madge merely snorted.

"Anyway, it seems that half of Devon's police force, including Moorcroft, is down with a 'flu-like bug."

"I thought the station was a bit quiet," Laurie said. "Might explain why the country's worst DS was sent out here, as well."

"The upshot is," my uncle continued, "there's no one competent to take this case on." He looked sternly at Laurie, daring him to make another inappropriate remark about a fellow officer. Laurie took the hint.

"The initial report indicates that the remains are of a middle-aged female. By the wear of her teeth, about forty years of age."

Laurie whistled. "So, not Colette?"

"So, not Colette," Uncle Toby confirmed, "which means, DS Walker, that you are, unless proven otherwise, innocent of any suspicion regarding her disappearance."

"Although that does leave things as an open case," I said, a little churlishly. I'd had the very selfish thought that, with Colette dead, I wouldn't have to worry about her relationship with Laurie any more. But then, there was still the awful sister to take into account.

"It's not the case I'm to be involved with," Uncle Toby said, "although I do wonder if all these circumstances are connected. When exactly did you last see Colette?"

Laurie frowned. "I've been trawling my brain about this. I took her to Umberleigh station, watched her walk onto the platform then drove off."

"So you didn't see her get on the train?"

"No."

"Anyone else there? Anyone else likely to have seen her?"

"That's what I've been trying to remember," Laurie admitted. "I'm fairly certain I saw Reverend Passwith's car in the car park. It's stuck in my mind because he was mending a puncture and I felt guilty at not offering to help – but, to be honest, I'm not sure if it was that day or the week before when I'd dropped Mum off at the station. Her monthly meeting with her ladies' group down at Eggesford."

My uncle frowned thoughtfully. "If it had been the week before, you wouldn't have been in such a rush to get off on your journey, would you? So, the week before you might have stopped to help with the tyre?"

Laurie looked relieved. "You're right! I would have done – so, yes, it must have been that day!"

"But of what significance is the pig?" Gran asked.

"No significance at all, except as an insult to the police," Laurie replied.

"Or a challenge," Aunt Madge proposed.

"Or a warning?" I said, worried. My aunt raised an eyebrow, gave me a surreptitious significant look, knowing exactly what I meant. My father, also a policeman, had been shot dead when I was a young child. I'd seen it happen.

All Uncle Toby answered with his usual non-committal, "*Mmm hmmm.*"

"The question is," Gran mused, "is it mere coincidence the two items being there, or are they connected?"

"Given the unpleasantness from the Haywoods, the pig was undoubtedly meant as an insult. Leaving that aside, we have two possibilities for an identity," Laurie said, thinking aloud. "Colette's mother disappeared without trace several years ago, and Reverend Passwith's wife apparently upped and left at the same time as Colette vanished."

"Or the victim could be someone entirely different," Gran pointed out.

"Two potentially murdered women is quite enough to be dealing with, thank you, Gran," Laurie responded, with what I thought was a very tolerant smile.

"Or maybe they're not dead?" I said. "They just left?"

"Possibly," Laurie answered, his smile more genuine this time, "but as we do have some unidentified remains..."

"Or," Aunt Madge interrupted, "we could leave the speculation to the local police, change the subject, and start enjoying Christmas Eve?"

"Um, sorry, afraid not." Her husband had the decency to look sheepish. "I hadn't quite finished what

I'd started saying. As I'm here for a week, Moorcroft has asked me to take the case on. Special circumstances and all that."

Aunt Madge, myself and Laurie all answered at once. In different ways.

Aunt. "Oh no, Toby! We're on holiday!"

Me. "Oh no, Uncle, we'll see nothing of you!"

Laurie. "Oh good. Where do we start?"

Gran also made a comment. "Is there any more tea?" But we ignored her.

"It's only for a few days *after* Christmas, Madge," Uncle Toby explained, "until a few personnel get back on their feet. We won't be able to do much these next couple of days anyway, and..."

Gran said, "And as those bones have clearly been bones for quite a while, there really is not much of a rush, is there?" She smiled and thanked Aunt Madge who was making her fresh tea. "Meanwhile, we can talk over what we have got, and present our conclusions to your Superintendent Moorcroft when he's stopped sniffling."

"Except," Uncle Toby replied, "we haven't got much to present him with."

Gran smiled. I noticed that she could put on a very sweet, condescending smile when she wanted to. "So, we had better get off our backsides and gather some more then, had we not?"

Laurie stretched and clasped his hands behind his head, his long legs sticking out from where he sat at the table. "So, what *have* we got?"

"A pile of bones in an old sack. Female, aged about forty." I said.

"A pig's head that coincidentally appeared on the compost heap the morning after two other pigs ravaged the garden," Gran contributed. "I think the porcine element is definitely relevant."

Uncle Toby partially agreed. "I do, indeed, think it was placed there as some sort of message – and a message for you, Laurie, unless anyone else knew I would be coming here for Christmas?"

Aunt Madge leant across the table to touch my hand. "We all kept it very secret as a surprise for Jan."

My uncle nodded; continued, "Moorcroft, through his coughing and spluttering, told me the pathologist mentioned teeth marks on the bones."

"Pigs?" Laurie said, lowering his arms to accept more coffee from Aunt Madge. "They'll eat anything, human flesh, leather, clothing. It wouldn't be the first time someone decided to dispose of a corpse in such a gruesome way."

"But I assume they cannot consume the larger bones? Skull, tibia, fibula, pelvis and so on," Gran queried. "Those will have to be disposed of elsewhere."

"Like in someone's compost heap," Laurie concluded.

I grimaced. It was all a bit horrid for Christmas Eve, to be honest.

"Shall I track down the pathologist, see if he's got anything more specific to tell us?" Laurie asked my uncle.

"No, I'll do that, I need to collect what information the station has anyway. You know the locals better than I, you could have an ask around, see if you can discover anything new about the missing women. All three of them."

"I'll start with the Haywoods, then, shall I?"

My uncle nodded. "I should."

"Well, if you are going into town, Toby," Aunt Madge declared, "I'll come with you. I just need to tidy this kitchen first; there's some last minute shopping to be done – I noticed Elsie hasn't got all the things I use for cooking Christmas dinner." She paused, looked aghast for a moment, then said to Laurie, "Your mother won't mind me taking over her kitchen, will she?"

Laurie laughed. "She'll be mortified because you are a guest, and guests don't cook their own meals – but she will, I suspect, also be most grateful because I've no idea how she'll manage turkey and all the trimmings with one arm in a plaster cast."

"And the rest of us will be delighted because, perhaps, we'll have an edible Christmas dinner for a change."

No one answered Gran's comment.

20

A BIT OF A SMELL

I half expected Gran to want to come with us to visit the Haywoods at Upper Valley View – she had already declined to go shopping with Aunt Madge.

"Goodness, no," she exclaimed when Laurie asked if she wanted to walk up the lane with us, "my days of trudging up these steep Devon hills are well past. I've plenty to occupy myself here."

"I'll light the sitting room fire for you, then," Laurie offered, "if you're sure?"

"Very sure," Gran insisted, "I'm half way through Simenon's *La Folle de Maigret,* so I'll be *plus de contenu, merci.*"

"*Très bien, grand-mère.*"

I was hopeless at French, so had no idea what they were saying. I smiled, though, and uttered the only French I could remember from school. "*Oui!*"

Well, in all honesty, I also remembered *ouvre la porte* but 'open the door' wasn't exactly appropriate.

"Is she really reading Maigret in French?" I whispered to Laurie as we left the house.

"*Naturellement.* She's fluent in several languages. Including Russian."

"Oh. Jolly good," I answered, feeling about as clever as an illiterate ant.

There didn't appear to be anyone at home when we knocked at the Haywoods' back door. (I'd already realised that very few people in the country used *front* doors when making an informal visit.) Borrowing the idea from Reverend Passwith, I'd made the suggestion that we could take Bess for a walk and drop in a Christmas card to the Haywoods, so, all apparently innocent, except Laurie said they never exchanged cards, so we dropped that bit and just used Bess instead.

I enjoyed the walk up the lane, and remarked that it must look lovely in spring and summer. Even this early (late?) there were a few primroses braving the smattering of snow.

"Primroses are very hardy," Laurie explained, "some clumps have been in situ for over fifty years, re-seeding and regenerating. There'll be foxgloves, stitchwort, columbine, cranesbill, ragged robin, dog roses and such; come next summer... Loads of daffodils in spring."

"But daffs are not wild flowers, are they? How do they get there in the first place?"

"Many that you see at the side of busy roads were planted to mark the spot of fatal accidents, but these lane daffodils originate from the Second World War."

I must have looked puzzled, because he laughed and squeezed my hand that I'd nestled snuggly in his. "Pre-war, Devon and Cornwall were noted for growing daffodils which were sent up to London's Covent Garden overnight by train. Then the war came and every field that was suitable had to be turned over for growing food – human or animal. The daff bulbs had to be dug up, but, rather than destroy them, many growers dispersed them among the hedgerows. They've been there, quietly multiplying, ever since."

"I can't imagine someone like Mr Haywood being all sentimental and scattering his daffs," I remarked as we tied Bess's lead to the farmyard gate at Higher Valley View and walked into the main yard – avoiding as much of the muck as we could. I was glad Laurie had suggested we don wellington boots.

"Mr Haywood?" Laurie called, several times. No response.

We walked to the nearest dilapidated building, a block of what had once been stables, but were now in various states of broken doors, crumbling walls and holed roofs. Ivy, bramble and weeds filled most of the gaps. Laurie continued to call out. We still received no answer. The furthest, end, stable – the only one which looked relatively solid and intact – had a front 'wall' of chicken wire and it stank of something pungent. As we got closer, my eyes started to water, the stink was so strong.

There were about fifteen or so lithe and sinuous animals inside the pen, climbing up the wire or playing on logs and branches scattered inside. There was quite a bit of debris as well: a shredded blanket, the remains of an old leather shoe, a headless teddy bear with its stuffing spilling out. (I made a mental note to ensure that Bee Bear was safe at home.)

I thought the creatures with their long, thin bodies and tiny eyes could be weasels or stoats; Laurie corrected me.

"These are ferrets from the family of carnivores which include weasels, badgers, otters and mink."

I giggled. "Aunt Madge used to have a mink coat, I hated it because it smelled."

A voice behind us made me jump. "Reeked o' mothballs, I expec'. What you two snoopers want?"

Chloë.

I swallowed down my revulsion as she sauntered to the smelly wire pen, opened the door and tossed in the two, whole, dead rabbits she was holding. The ferrets went barmy. I had to turn away because they pounced on the rabbits – not exactly a pretty sight.

"They've got t'eat," Chloë said, noticing my expression.

I didn't say anything, although I wanted to say, 'Yes, but so savagely?' From the way the creatures were squabbling, I reckoned it wouldn't take them long to devour their breakfast.

"The toys are for 'em t'play with. They get bored, else. An' they'll eat everythin' they're given," Chloë explained, "fur, skin, bone. It don't take 'em long t'strip a rabbit or chicken carcass."

I managed what I hoped was a congenial smile. "What, like pigs do?"

"They eat anythin'. Dead or alive. So, watch y'fingers."

"Mum's not very happy about her wrecked garden," Laurie said, changing the subject.

"Seems t'me that them coppers made far more mess than did our hogs."

"Maybe so, but you must make sure that your pigs are kept behind secure fencing in future. And no leaving gates open."

"What pigs you talkin' 'bout?" Chloë challenged. "Ain't got no pigs now. Went off to make your sausages an' bacon early this mornin'. This lot," she pointed to the ferrets, are goin' t'morrer. I've sold 'em to some chap in next village."

"You had four pigs last time I was here? And you're fond of your ferrets, why sell them?" Laurie said, not quite as questions, but not quite statements either.

"The two other hogs went a couple o' days ago.

Same reason as why this lot are goin' – we ain't got no money. Anyways, why you askin'? Want some pork chops d'you?" She gave a toss of her hair, which I noticed would have benefitted from a good shampoo and combing. "Or maybe a nice pig's 'ead with an apple stuffed in its gob for Christmas dinner?"

Laurie narrowed his eyes, suspicious. "Happen to have had one handy to leave where it shouldn't have been left, eh?"

"No. The scraps are fer m'ferrets."

"So, it wasn't you who left us the gift of a pig's head?"

Chloë tossed her head again, her eyes flashed anger. I was sure I saw a louse in her hair.

"O' course not. Why would I do that?"

"To make a point? To have a go at me? Play a joke?"

"Damn stupid joke, givin' away m'ferret's dinner."

"All the same..."

"It's in 'ere," Chloë went to one of the other stables that had more rubble than solid walls. She lifted the lid of a rusty old metal corn bin. "It's in 'ere if'n you don't believe me!"

Laurie peered inside. "Nothing there. It's empty."

"What? 'Course it's there!" She elbowed Laurie aside, stared into the bin, then let rip with a colourful stream of expletives, all of which were directed at her 'drunken sot' of a father.

"I'll bloody kill him," she snarled. "He's a no good, lyin', murderin' thief! That were fer this lot."

"Where is he, your father?" Laurie asked.

"Don't know, don't care. Six foot under, with any luck."

"What about the wire?" I asked, "I suppose you're going to claim that it was him who strung a strand of wire across Mrs Walker's garden step?" I confronted her, angrily. "He could have broken Elsie's neck, not her arm! Or was it you who did it?"

"Nothin' t'do with me!" Chloë spat back.

I was rather proud of myself because I stood my ground, though I wanted to hide behind Laurie. "I don't believe you." I countered. "I saw you tucking wire into your pocket!"

"That were fer mendin' the bloody fence – the fence the hogs kept breakin' down!"

I still didn't believe her, but I couldn't prove that she was not telling the truth. All I could do was ask, "Well, who *did* set that wire?"

"I've no idea. Prob'ly Dad, like you said. Vicious sod. Sort o' thing 'e would do when 'e's in the foul mood 'e's in. Your Dad, Lawrence Walker, should never 'ave sacked 'im. We've no food, no money, no..."

"Save the sob story, Chloë," Laurie retaliated. "Your dad always finds enough money to spend on his beer and whisky. He could have caused a serious accident. Did he bury those bones as well?"

"What bones? I know nothin' about no bones. You tryin' t'pin summat else on me?"

Out of the blue, the anger changed and Chloë burst into tears. "I miss m'sister. I 'ate it 'ere with just 'im." Then she started punching at Laurie's chest and shoulders. "You tryin' t'get me in trouble like you got our Colly in trouble back in the spring? When you got 'er in the family way!"

I stared at Laurie. He didn't look back at me, but I could see his neck and face turning as red as beetroot juice.

He grasped Chloë's wrists to fend her blows off. "You know that isn't true, Chloë."

Through gulps of tears she shouted, "Ain't it? I saw y'both more than once sneakin' into our barn fer a bit o' 'ow's y'father!"

"That you did not, because we did not. Now, stop this!"

Laurie succumbed to the crocodile tears and put his arm round Chloë's shoulders.

I'd seen and heard enough. "I think Bess is whining," I lied, and turning on my heals (not elegantly done, wellies don't lend themselves to elegance) and marched back to the lane.

I heard Chloë, the tears suddenly dried up, snigger. "I didn't 'ear no dog. Tells porkies often, do she?"

Hah! She could talk!

Back at the gate, I let Bess off her lead and started back down the lane, wiping away a tear or two of my own as I walked. It was stupid to cry – I was well aware I was being silly – but what if the wretched girl wasn't making up all that about her sister? What if Laurie *had* got this wretched Colette pregnant?

I heard footsteps hurrying behind me. I kept walking. A hand grabbed my arm, spun me around. I almost slipped on an icy patch of snow.

"Let me go. Leave me alone!" I snapped, trying to shrug Laurie off.

"No, I won't, you silly girl. You don't seriously believe that little madam, do you? About any of it? She excels at causing trouble, that one. Always has done. Takes after her damned father."

He gave my arm a shake as I tried again to pull away from his grip.

"It isn't true, Jan! I've never been in a barn – or anywhere – with Colly, well apart from the cinema and a pub or two. The most I did was give her a goodnight kiss – on her cheek, Jan, on her *cheek*!"

I didn't answer, I just brushed at the tears that were trickling down my face.

Laurie moved my fingers aside and wiped the tears

with his thumb. "Listen, love, do you really believe her, and not me?"

I didn't answer because a car appeared around the bend, Uncle Toby's Jaguar. He pulled to a halt and wound the driver's side window down; I turned away, pretending to look for something in my coat pocket so that he wouldn't see I'd been crying.

"Would you be willing to come with me, Sergeant Walker? I'd like to have a word with the Umberleigh stationmaster. I believe you know him?"

"I do indeed, sir, but I'm not exactly dressed for formal interviews." He indicated his mucky wellingtons.

"I've brought a decent pair of shoes for you to change into," Aunt Madge called from the passenger seat.

"And its informal, not formal," Uncle Toby added. "You won't mind if we steal him away for an hour or so, will you, Jan?"

I had to answer him, so as I turned round I fixed a smile to my face. "No, of course not. I can keep Gran company, or is there anything I can do in the kitchen for you, Aunt Madge?"

"No, dear, just make Elsie and Alf a cup of tea when they get home."

"Right ho!" I responded, sounding cheerful. "Come on, Bess, home!"

I marched off down the lane, not looking at, or saying a word to, Laurie.

21

INTERLUDE: LAURIE

It was all very awkward as I settled myself on the back seat of DCI Christopher's very posh car. It smelled of expensive leather and car polish – and I hoped, after I'd taken off my boots and placed them carefully on the newspaper that Mrs Christopher had thoughtfully put down, that pig muck wasn't adding to the aroma.

We drove up the lane in silence, turned onto the main road which was, basically, a wider lane, heading for the main road proper that would take us to Barnstaple.

"Everything all right?" my boss asked.

"Yes, sir, fine." It was an odds-on bet that he knew I was lying.

"Get anything useful from the Haywoods?"

"No, nothing, except they'd sent a couple of their pigs to the abattoir a few days ago. Could be where they got the pig's head from? I'm fairly convinced it was Chloë who left it for us, but she says it was her father. It's the sort of unfunny joke she would pull, though."

DCI Christopher waited for a tractor to trundle over

the bridge at Umberleigh, then, following my directions, drove on. "No proof either way?"

"Not unless forensics can lift any fingerprints – which is highly unlikely."

"This is all very pretty!" Mrs Christopher declared waving her hand towards the view. "I've always loved it here in Devon."

We took the hint and changed the subject away from police matters.

Dropping Mrs C in Tuly Street, outside the old buildings of Dornat's Mineral Water Works, we arranged to meet her in the corner café in an hour, and drove on to the police station. DCI Christopher suggested that I wait in the car, so I transferred to the driver's seat while he went in to collect what files and information he could scrummage up – I always drove for him back in Chingford; saw no reason not to change the habit now.

When he emerged from the police station, he put a couple of folders in the boot and sighed as he made himself comfortable in the passenger seat. He took his hat off (he always wore a hat, a US-style Fedora, a favourite of his wife's apparently) and flicked it onto the back seat. He rested his head back, closed his eyes and sighed.

"I see what you mean regarding DS Frobisher."

I kept what I wanted to reply to myself. It was most unusual for my boss to make any sort of comment about a fellow officer. But I understood why he had. Frobisher would try the patience of all the saints and apostles combined.

"Did you manage to get what files were available from him, sir?"

"I did. Wrestling a crocodile would have been easier. And more desirable." He opened his eyes, part-grinned. "And I never said that. Understood?"

"Understood, sir. The station? The other station, that is. Railway?"

"I think so, don't you?"

He closed his eyes again, murmured, "What a shame we can't pin this murder on Frobisher. There would be some great satisfaction in doing so."

I knew exactly what he meant.

———

We found Mr Simmons on the platform at the station, gazing down the track at the rear end of the train departing for Exeter.

We both showed our ID and DCI Christopher outlined our enquiry.

"Colette Haywood? Aye, her disappearance is still a mystery, isn't it?" Mr Simmons said, "but I'll not be able to help. I were transferred here to Barnstaple long before May, when the previous stationmaster retired, and Umberleigh, well, let's just say 'changed'."

I could hear the regret in his voice. That period must have been upsetting for him and his family – for all the railway workers, come to that, especially those who were unfortunate enough to lose their jobs.

"My wife might have been there," he added. "A Saturday, you say? She often went down to tend the plants on Saturdays. Shall I ask her to join us for a cuppa?"

Happy to chat for a few minutes, he escorted us into his station master's office and called his wife on the telephone, then offered us tea. I accepted, DCI Christopher declined.

Living in a house opposite the station, Mrs Simmons soon arrived.

"So, how can I help you gentlemen?" she asked, going straight away to pour boiling water from the kettle that had been simmering on a very old-fashioned Aga, that I wouldn't have minded wagering had been put in when the station was first built in the late 1800s. Though I doubt they had Agas back then, so I am slightly exaggerating.

"Do you recall anything about Colette Haywood being at Umberleigh Station last May, just before she disappeared?" I asked, while getting out my notebook in case there was anything useful to write down.

"Goodness, now you be askin', young Laurie." She smiled. "Beg pardon, Detective Sergeant!" Holding her own cup of tea, she seated herself in the only armchair, which I guessed her husband occupied a lot of the time, for there was a newspaper folded open at a half-finished crossword on a table next to it.

"Now, let me think," she continued. "I do remember the day because, as it happened, our son was off to Lunnon on that same train. He helped Reverend Passwith's wife into the carriage. Poor dear was all a-fluster, upset about something, though I don't know what."

"Where was she going? Do you know?"

She shook her head. "Exeter, mebbe? Or transferrin' to the Lunnon train at Exeter St David's."

"And Miss Haywood?" DCI Christopher prompted.

"Ah, now that I can tell you. She flounced on to the platform in a right bad mood she were. Waited till the last moment to board, but then changed her mind – just walked off, leaving the carriage door wide open. Right dangerous. I called out to her and told her what I thought – one of the passengers had to lean out to shut it. Could have been a nasty accident."

I exchanged a glance with my boss. So, Colly had never set off to London.

"Do you know where she went?" I asked carefully, barely daring to breathe.

"Why, aye, I do. I remember because, if I'd had the chance, I would have given her a piece of my mind. She ran into the carpark and got into someone's car. Well, I assume she did, because she weren't there when I got there, and I did hear a car race off."

I exchanged a glance with DCI Christopher.

"Do you happen to know whose car?" he asked.

Of course, life would have been too simple had she replied *Yes*. All she could tell us was that the car was white with a noisy exhaust. Not much help at all, except Reverend Passwith's car had been in the carpark. And it was white. And it had an exhaust problem. Everyone in the village knew when the vicar was coming because of the *phut-phut-phut* noise.

Needless to say, when we later called at the reverend's house in the village, neither he nor his housekeeper were at home, not that anyone in the village knew for certain that she *was* his housekeeper. Gossip was rife, but gossip was not always accurate. So that put paid to any investigation until after Christmas.

I can't say that I minded too much.

We'd collected Mrs Christopher and her shopping, and, bless her, she'd bought two huge bouquets of flowers for me to give to Jan and Mum. She hadn't said anything but had obviously guessed that Jan and I'd had a tiff.

"My niece and your mother need not know that you didn't buy them yourself," she advised.

I apologised to Jan as soon as we got home, and was relieved when she forgave me. I'd been an idiot, I should have told her more about Colette, but there had truly been *nothing* in *that* nature between us. I should have anticipated Chloë being such an obnoxious cat, though.

Mum was home, looking pale and wan. (As they say in books.) She'd gone straight to bed so I plonked her flowers in a vase – re-arranged by Jan – and took them up to her room, but she was feeling better by dinner time. We ate a fantastic meal by candlelight, accompanied by a couple of bottles of red wine and a good bit of laughter. Us men insisted on clearing the table and doing the washing up – which in turn was accompanied by even more laughter and more wine. We only broke two plates. The ladies made themselves comfortable in the sitting room, and after we'd served coffee laced with brandy, I tickled the piano for a little while so we could have a sing-song – a few carols, but mostly old-time favourites – then we played cards until bedtime. I swear my boss cheated, because he won more hands than anyone else.

Our pre-bed Christmas ritual was to bring out the wrapped presents from their various hiding places and pile them beneath the tree ready for Christmas morning.

"But I thought Father Christmas delivered them?" Jan teased.

"He burnt his bum badly on the Yule Log one year when he came down the chimney," I explained with a straight face, "so he now insists on leaving them here earlier." We laughed and I hugged her, gave her a Christmas kiss. I'd left a package for her on her pillow, wrapped in shiny paper with a note on the label: *Not to be opened until Christmas morning. I'll be questioning the bear to make sure you don't cheat. I love you.*

I envied that bear. He got to be cuddled all night.

I'd have given anything to swap places.

22

CHRISTMAS INTRUSION

Even at eighteen years old (soon to be nineteen) I still awoke early on Christmas morning with that tingly feeling of anticipated excitement. I guess most of us do. Deep inside, we cherish that hope for a special day with lots of nice things happening. Although I'm aware that it often doesn't end up like that for many people. Too much to drink, not enough money, over-hyped expectation. Family rows that can lead to violence. That's the truth for many, but even so, I woke up looking forward to the day, enhanced by the wrapped package from Laurie that I'd put under my pillow.

I had been tempted to open it soon after I'd snuggled into bed and heard the clock downstairs chime midnight – I'd even got as far as tugging at the ribbon bound around it, but then remembered that the clock was always ten-minutes fast, so I put my gift back under the pillow, and promptly fell asleep until 6.30 a.m.

The rest of the house was quiet. I switched on the bedside light and eagerly unwrapped the present. It was expensive. Chanel No. 5 Perfume. Indulgent, I dabbed a little on my wrists and behind my ears and asked Bee Bear what he thought. He was still asleep, so didn't answer. For fun, I dabbed a little on his nose.

I dozed until eight o'clock when I heard movement, got up, got dressed. Breakfast, Happy Christmas wishes and kisses to everyone. (Laurie grinned and said I smelled nice.) Church for morning carols, with the turkey cooking in the Aga, and a glorious aroma filling the house when we came home. We had coffee after 'all hands' had helped peel the spuds and top-'n'-tail the sprouts. All hands except Elsie whom we insisted must put her feet up in the sitting room. She protested, exclaiming that she really shouldn't expect guests to cook their own dinner, but we – Uncle Toby and myself – assured her that Aunt Madge was in her element; she loved cooking, particularly special meals on special occasions, for special people.

One present each from the tree. Laurie handed them out. We had given Gran and Elsie their hyacinths at breakfast, with me apologising to Aunt Madge that had I known she was coming...! She only laughed and said that the box of gifts I'd left at home for her and my uncle were now piled with the rest. "We brought them with us, dear!"

As Laurie had predicted, Gran had wrinkled her nose at her plants. "How am I to get these home, then?" she complained.

Alf muttered, "In a basket on the back of your broomstick," but I don't think she heard, or at least, she ignored him.

"We can take you home, Gran," Laurie offered. "Maidenhead isn't out of our way."

Gran frowned. "What? In that rusty old car of yours? No, thank you. Besides, I have paid for a return railway ticket."

I opened a little present labelled *'With love from Elsie'* and I laughed when I discovered what it was. A tiny, exquisitely knitted black and yellow striped jumper for Bee Bear.

"I asked your aunt what you'd like as a 'smiley' present – we always give each other something to make us smile, nothing practical, nothing useful or expensive. I hope it fits him?"

I rushed upstairs to fetch him, put his new jumper on and brought him downstairs to show everyone. "Perfect fit!" I announced.

Funnily enough, my present to Laurie was a jumper, a somewhat larger one, of course, a traditional Irish Aran in the customary off-white báinín colour, with cable patterns on the body and sleeves. I had an Irish friend who knitted them, and just as Elsie had found out about the size for Bee Bear, I'd found out Laurie's size from Elsie. What a surreptitious lot we can be at Christmas!

We gave Alf the photograph album, which he was delighted with, but didn't get a chance to more than quickly glance at, as it was time for us 'able bodied' to help in the kitchen. Elsie was firmly told to sit by the fire and start the novel her husband had given her – the hardback edition of *The Dwelling Place* by Catherine Cookson. Gran Ethel (making a remark about trite fiction) picked up the photograph album and started browsing through. No one disturbed her – for once she seemed approving and contented. Photographs obviously counted as acceptable, alongside French novels. And then it was time to carve the turkey, and serve Christmas Dinner.

Aunt Madge had done us proud, and we all flopped into the comfort of the sitting room to recover from being over-stuffed with good food and wine. Laurie was too full to even consider playing the piano again. I've no idea who fell almost instantly asleep because I was one of the first to doze off, my head on Laurie's shoulder, his arm around my waist as we curled up together on one of the settees. Bess barking woke us all up.

It must have been about 3.15 – we all felt guilty at missing the Queen's speech on TV – Bess barked again, and there came a loud knock at the front door.

"Who on earth has come calling on Christmas Day?" Alf asked rhetorically as he heaved himself up and headed for the hall. We were all astonished a moment later when he came back with Reverend Passwith in tow.

"I do apologise for disturbing your afternoon, I forgot to drop off a Christmas card the other day, and I wondered how you were, Mrs Walker? I heard you'd had a nasty accident – and I believe you left me a note, wanting to see me Mr Christopher? Something about you are looking into Colette Haywood's disappearance?"

My uncle, polite as always, had risen to his feet, held out his hand. "Detective Chief Inspector Christopher. I'm pleased to meet you, Reverend, but, as it's my day off, I'm quite happy to wait until another day – unless you can confirm that you gave Colette Haywood a lift from Umberleigh station on the day she went missing back in May?"

The Reverend frowned. "May? That was a while ago now, wasn't it?"

"I'm fine," Elsie said answering his first enquiry, brandishing her plaster cast as she also got to her feet. We'd all signed it and drawn Christmassy motifs with coloured pens to make it look festive. "A simple fracture, nothing of much consequence."

"Glad to hear it, glad to hear it," the reverend beamed.

"Maybe Miss Haywood is not a suitable subject for Christmas Day?" Aunt Madge interrupted, glaring at her husband and the reverend in turn.

Reverend Passwith failed to take the hint. "I told all to the police at the time; my statement must be on file somewhere."

"We like to look at things afresh where we can," Laurie responded, going to stand beside my uncle. The intrusion was becoming all too – well, intrusive.

The reverend nodded. "I see. I did, indeed, give her a lift. She was in a bit of a pickle from what I recall. She'd just got off the train from Barnstaple, and had been let down or something. I dropped her in the village."

"I don't think that's..." Laurie began.

Uncle interrupted him, "Not quite what we have been led to believe, but perhaps we can have a deeper discussion after the Christmas festivities?"

"Of course, of course, but that is what the young lady told me. That she'd come from Barnstaple and needed to get home; but if you wish to go through my statement again later? Now that I am no longer a practicing vicar, I have plenty of time on my hands. On my own for Christmas and all that."

As a hint it was pretty broad.

"I thought your housekeeper lived with you?" Elsie remarked.

"My housekeeper? Oh, no, she's... well, she is visiting friends today."

A moment of silence, broken by Elsie whose conscience got the better of her. "I'm about to make tea for us all, Reverend, please do say you'll have a cup? Can I take your coat?"

Laurie exchanged a discreet look with his dad. What possessed the woman!

"You stay where you are, Elsie, I'll make the tea," I offered.

"Nonsense, I'm quite capable of putting the kettle on, but you can help with carrying things, pet, if you would."

The reverend sat down on the nearest settee next to Gran, who had the photograph album open on her lap.

"Oh," he said peering at the page nearest to him, "The Acropolis, is it not? One place I would dearly like to see. Athens, the Greek Islands, all that magnificent culture."

"It's not all it's cracked up to be," Gran sniffed, closed the album and put it behind her.

Polite small talk followed for more than half an hour, stilted conversation about nothing important. The reverend asked if he could smoke, which I thought was a cheek in someone else's house, but Laurie provided him with an ashtray. Elsie finally announced that the tea cups and plates (we'd also indulged in slices of rich fruit Christmas cake) needed clearing away. We all sprang to help, apart from Alf who decided Bess needed a run in the garden, and the hens shutting away. Even Gran collected up a couple of cups. In the hall, Laurie handed our unwelcome guest, who had taken the hint, his coat. He folded it over his arm, then patted his jacket pocket.

"Dear me, I think I've left my cigarettes on the settee ... no, no I'll fetch them!"

He was gone but a moment, bid us goodbye and at last, left.

"Huh! 'housekeeper' indeed!" Elsie declared scornfully. "His bit of stuff, if you ask me!"

"Mum!" Laurie chided, "Lots of vicars have housekeepers."

She merely snorted.

"How about the rest of our presents?" Alf suggested, standing before the fire to get warm – it was bitter cold outside. And thank goodness now that the reverend was gone, no longer as 'cold' indoors!

23

BOXING DAY

The trouble with Christmas is that a lot happens in a
short space of time and then 'poof' it's all over for
another year. We were late up to bed – I say 'we', Elsie
and Gran went up at about ten, the rest of us said
goodnight at not far off midnight after a devious game
of Monopoly. I think Alf won, although I swear he
cheats at these things as much as my uncle does.
Monopoly is one of those board games that you either
love or hate. I enjoy it as long as no one takes it
seriously. I also suggest that playing while sharing
several bottles of something alcoholic between the
players puts a completely different slant on the game –
mainly, a lot of good-natured laughter. And as a bonus,
the state of mild inebriation results in no one disputing
the winner the next morning, because no one will
clearly remember anything

I lay in bed for a while, again listening to the
sounds of the house settling to sleep. On my bedside
cabinet the bottle of Chanel stood next to the wooden
owl that I'd admired at the Pannier Market in South
Molton. Laurie had somehow managed to buy it
without me noticing. It was gorgeous. Laurie was

gorgeous. In fact, it had been a gorgeous Christmas Day, although there had been two minor hiccups. The reverend's uninvited visit mid-afternoon had been a little embarrassing and boring, and, come our eventual bedtime, Alf couldn't find his photograph album, although as we (a bit giggly) had pointed out, we were all 'tiddly', so not capable of searching thoroughly. And anyway, it was probable that Gran had taken it up to bed with her.

"Old bat would steal her own grandmother if it suited her," Alf had whispered (loudly) as we'd trooped upstairs. "I ought to call a policeman!" he'd added.

"Call a policeman what?" Aunt Madge had laughed, which set us all off again.

Elsie had come out from her bedroom to shush us all.

"You're making enough noise to waken the dead!" she hissed.

"Not Gran, then?" Alf had responded.

More laughter.

And no, I didn't have a hangover when I woke up. Well, not much of one. Nothing an Alka Seltzer wouldn't sort out.

A penpal friend of mine who lives in North Carolina told me in one of her letters that they didn't celebrate Boxing Day in the USA. I suppose it is a traditional English custom that didn't get taken over to America with the *Mayflower*. Mind you, the US has Thanksgiving, which we don't, so *quid pro quo*. Or should that be *quo vadis*? (I'm not very good at Latin.) Or is that something like *wither goest thou?* a quote from the Bible?

Anyway... Boxing Day was another bright, sunny, but cold morning. Unanimously, we decided to go for an adventure, so we donned boots and coats and bundled into Alf and Uncle Toby's cars to drive up onto Exmoor. It was glorious up there! We parked near Dunkery Beacon first of all, and trooped up to the summit, a sandstone hill, rising to not far off two thousand feet, the highest point in North Devon. The view was spectacular, looking out across the surrounding moorland and the Bristol Channel. The Moors were every shade of green and brown, while the sea sparkled a deep blue with white horses galloping headlong with the tide.

My aunt is a part-time watercolour painter (she's very good) and had captured almost the exact same view when she was here with Uncle Toby on their honeymoon. The picture hangs in the hall back home. I was thrilled to see the real scenery!

Laurie told us that Bronze Age and Iron Age people had lived up on Dunkery, all I could say, they must have been hardy souls, for the westerly wind, coming straight off the sea, was very strong and very cold.

We then motored to the Valley of the Rocks, another geological feature right on the cliffs above the sea. The Ice Age and coastal erosion had formed the huge, towering pillars of rock that looked like something out of a science fiction film, which, naturally, as I was writing a sci-fi novel immediately gave me the idea for an unearthly landscape to put my hero and his family in.

Apparently, the stunning formations were some of the oldest Devonian rocks and, according to the guide book I'd brought along, were 'highly fossiliferous'. I wasn't sure what that word meant, but I didn't like to ask anyone to explain in front of Gran, who was enthralled because William Wordsworth and Samuel Taylor Coleridge had visited this very spot in... whenever it was. I was more interested in the fact that R.D. Blackmore had set some scenes here for the most famous Exmoor heroine of all time, Lorna Doone. And then we were all laughing because of the sudden appearance of the Exmoor wild goat herd that are equally as famous.

We then found a sheltered spot to consume the picnic Aunt Madge had prepared: cold turkey sandwiches, ham sandwiches, sausage rolls, mince pies, Christmas cake. A doggie biscuit for Bess. Beer, lemonade... Stuffed full, we ought to have gone for a good walk after eating our way through that lot, but instead, we went home and fell asleep in front of the fire.

Lazy lot, I know, but what's Boxing Day for, if not for total relaxation?

24

ROOTLING

The holiday break didn't last long, not for Laurie and Uncle Toby, anyway. My Uncle had sent a note to Reverend Passwith, asking him to meet them at Barnstaple Police Station at 10.30 a.m, just to 'run through a few things', so they had left by the time I had got dressed and wandered, yawning, downstairs for some breakfast. I'd been disturbed in the night by shots echoing down the valley. I'd heard them before – a farmer out after rabbits or deer, Laurie had assured me. Nothing to worry about, a common sound in the countryside.

Elsie and Gran were still abed, and Alf had taken Bess for a long walk, a ploy to avoid his mother-in-law, I suspected.

"What say you to a little bit of rootling?" Aunt Madge proposed to me as I poured the last of the milk onto my cornflakes.

"Rootling?"

She grinned. "Finding out a few things."

"Deviously?"

"Very deviously."

I grinned. That sounded an interesting proposition.

"We can take a stroll up the lane to the village, visit the shop, then maybe call in at the reverend's to repay the compliment of his unexpected intrusion the other day."

"But he won't be there," I reminded her.

My Aunt has a wicked streak lurking beneath her benign exterior. "We know that, but his housekeeper won't know that we know, will she?"

We called in at the village shop first to buy fresh milk. Aunt Madge also bought three boxes of Devon made shortbread, although she hadn't intended to.

"We're going to Reverend Passwith's, hoping for morning coffee," she explained to the shopkeeper, who had introduced herself as Heather, after enquiring whether we were visitors or just passing through.

"You'll be lucky," Heather responded, "since he came back, no one's been invited near, let alone inside. Keeps himself to himself, does that man. Always did, even when he was our vicar."

Aunt Madge leant conspiratorially across the counter, lowered her voice, although there was no one else in the shop. "Well, he turned up at Valley View Farm on Christmas afternoon – invited himself in for tea and cake!"

Heather sighed, shook her head. "Doesn't surprise me. He's a 'taker' that one, expects everyone to kow-tow to what he wants. We weren't sorry to see him go, to tell the truth, though it meant the cottage was standing empty for months. Now, *Mrs* Passwith, she were a lovely lady. Took us all by surprise when she just upped an' went without a goodbye to a single soul. Nor never a word from her since."

"And he has a housekeeper now, I believe?" Aunt Madge was good at rootling out information.

Heather snorted and folded her arms. "If you want to call her that. There's only two bedrooms in that little house, you know, well, three if you count the tiny box room. It were a farm cottage, a bit on the derelict side when he first moved here back in," she frowned, thinking, "must have been 1960 or early '61, because he christened our girl in the summer of '61."

Neither Aunt Madge nor I cared to divert the interesting conversation by asking who 'our girl' was.

"They bought the cottage because they didn't want the vicarage; a rambling, draughty old place it were. Got sold by the diocese, rather than spend money on doing it up. It's a hotel now." She nodded towards me. "You must be Laurie's young lady? Heard all about you, we have. You mind you look to him, he's a good lad is our Laurie."

I assured her that I had every intention of doing so.

"Now," Heather said, pushing an expensive box of shortbread across the counter in our direction, "why not take along something nice in case you do get invited in for coffee? Shortbread's on special offer today. And maybe a box for Elsie, seeing as she's poorly?"

"What a good idea, thank you!" Aunt Madge enthused, taking a second box as well.

"What about a box for Gran?" I suggested.

"Another good idea. We'll have three boxes, please, Heather."

"Sold, to the lady in the rather nice blue Cashmere coat! Buy two for twenty pence, and get a third for the bargain price of just 10p." Heather chuckled at what I guessed was a regular joke of hers. (Work it out!)

We left the shop, trying very hard not to giggle.

"Now, that's what I call a good shopkeeper," Aunt Madge laughed, "selling things to customers who had no idea they wanted them!"

The reverend's house was the last-but-one at the end of the village High Street – a posh term for the main road, which wasn't much wider than Valley View's goat track of a lane, had no street lighting and a trail of sloppy, green cow pats crossing it leading from one field to another. A smartly dressed woman, a little older than Aunt Madge, who would never let on that she was just the wrong side of forty-five, answered the door. She looked vaguely familiar, although I couldn't place where I'd seen her before. At the carols round the bonfire, perhaps?

Madge immediately launched into her made-up spiel: "Oh, hello, we're looking for Reverend Passwith, is he at home?"

"I'm afraid not."

"Oh, well, never mind. Are you his housekeeper?" She didn't wait for an answer. "The reverend visited us the other day, so kind of him to call in – we're staying with friends at Valley View Farm, I expect you know them? Anyway, the dear soul borrowed a photograph album from us, but we've just realised we need it back, I wonder if you could find it?"

I managed to hide my look of utter surprise. How on earth...?

"You had better come in," the woman said, standing back from the door. "I'm not his housekeeper, though, I'm his sister-in-law."

"Oh, how do you do!" Madge held out her hand. "I'm Mrs Marjorie Christopher, and you are Beatrice Pye, of course. A delight to meet you. I follow all your recipes."

Ah, *that's* where I had seen the woman – on the back cover of quite a few cookery books and on BBC TV. She was a television personality cook and prolific writer of everything food related, from a variety of simple meals to luxury recipes, healthy diet and affordable nutrition.

Miss Pye took Madge's hand, then shook mine. "I'm Beatrice Norbutt in everyday life; please, do sit down." She indicated seats in the cosy front living room. There was a delicious aroma of baking bread coming from the kitchen. "I'll have a look in his room," Beatrice said. She disappeared and came back a moment later with Alf's photograph album.

"Is this the one?"

"Yes, thank you!" Aunt Madge took the album and tucked it under her arm. "Are you here to stay with the reverend? Such a pretty village, don't you think?"

Given the circumstances of what almost amounted to impertinent interrogation, Miss Norbutt answered most graciously. "No, this is my house; he is staying with me until New Year. Then, I am hoping he will be gone for good, but I could not, in my heart, see him left alone for Christmas. My elder sister, his wife, bought the cottage from money left to us by our father. In turn, she bequeathed me the place in her will. She passed away in July. Cancer. She'd been living with me in London so as to be near the big hospitals, all to no avail, alas."

"I'm so sorry," my aunt answered with genuine sympathy, "such an awful illness."

"Indeed. It always seems to take the nice people, not the rotters."

I had the distinct impression that by 'rotters' she meant Reverend Passwith. Which probably explained why he had not been left the house by his wife.

We exchanged a few more pleasantries, with my aunt enthusing about recipes and so forth, then took our leave.

"How on earth did you know he had the album?" I asked as we walked away from the cottage.

"Simple deduction, my dear. The album was there

before our visitor arrived. He showed great interest in it. He left. Album was gone."

I laughed. "Does Uncle Toby know how clever you are?"

"I remind him frequently."

25

IDENTITIES

"Ah you found the album then?" Gran observed as we walked into the kitchen at Valley View. She was making tea, indicated the pot to see if we wanted a cup and was grateful for the milk. "Where was it? With that odious vicar, I assume."

"I'll have coffee," Madge answered, as she poured some milk into a jug, put the glass bottles in the fridge, then the boxes of shortbread on the table and slid one across to Gran. "For you."

"I'll take one up to Elsie, shall I?" I offered.

"She's in the sitting room, not upstairs. No idea where Alfred has got to. He's never around when you want him," Gran grumbled.

"Do you want him?" Aunt Madge said with a smile, "or are things a lot easier with him out of the way?"

Gran laughed. "Quite right. They only get under out feet. Now then, let's see why the Black Crow wanted this album, shall we?"

It didn't take her long to flick through the photographs and point to one in particular, the small wedding party that I had noticed when I was looking through the album in the Pannier Market. The background was a neo-Gothic Victorian building.

"Is that the Natural History Museum in London?" I asked, hoping to appear clever at recognising it.

Ethel put me right. "It's the Oxford University Museum of Natural History. I'll no doubt have to repeat all this to DCI Christopher," she said, "but while we three ladies are sitting here...This," she pointed to the bride, "is Judith Mallard. I don't know who the other woman is – although as she is the same woman in all the photographs, I would assume the photographer is her husband, brother, father or lover."

"Or a 'woman' friend?" Aunt Madge suggested. "Maybe that is why the photographer is always secreted behind the camera, not in front of it?"

Being somewhat naïve about a few things in the world, especially euphemism where 'relationships' were concerned, I didn't quite understand her meaning, but I let it pass.

"Hmm, possible. Irrelevant, though. This man," Ethel pointed to the taller of the two males, who sported a bushy beard and looked as sour as vinegar, "is our Reverend Passwith, before he became a reverend."

Now that she'd said, I could see that she was right. I pointed to the bride. "She looks familiar. Have we seen her before?"

"Not her no, but she is remarkably like her youngest daughter who lives at the top of the lane."

"Judith Mallard is Mrs Haywood!" I exclaimed, "Chloë and Colette's mother?"

"*Was* Mrs Haywood. Or believed was, at any rate," Gran corrected.

"So, the newlywed husband here, must be Godfrey Haywood?" Madge queried.

"Correct. Although, if I recall, the smiles were false."

"You knew them?"

"I did, well, I knew Judith. She was one of our girls at Bletchley. She stayed on in a different department as a filing clerk after the war, kept in touch, especially when she discovered that she was four months pregnant and didn't know which one of her two lovers was the father. Not that it mattered, because the one who was about to be ordained wouldn't consider marriage because 'people would talk'. Haywood didn't have the same reservations, but then he desperately wanted a son to please *his* father, and to pass the family farm on to. Neither of them were aware, at the time, that Judith was intimate with them both. I've no idea when, or if, they ever found out."

"I suppose Haywood was disappointed that the child was a girl?" Aunt Madge observed.

"And has been disappointed ever since?" I added. "I wonder if Chloë Haywood knows that the reverend could have been her sister's father?"

"I would say not," my aunt answered, "which is why he took the album, in case anyone who shouldn't see the photo did see it."

"But how did he know *we* had it?" Gran tossed in.

I felt rather pleased that I knew the answer. "I bought it at the Pannier Market, from a man who did house clearance, which usually happens after someone dies – presumably the person who owned this album; either the woman in the photographs, or the photographer. Our reverend told Chloë that he had asked her father to buy him something from the market, only Mr Haywood spent the money on drink, instead. I reckon he was supposed to have bought this album."

"Not that this tells us which poor soul ended up on Alfred's compost heap," Gran remarked.

"Oh, but I think we do know," Aunt Madge said. "It isn't the reverend's wife. She died in a London hospital a few months ago. Toby said the teeth belonged to an older woman, so it isn't Colette, which leaves us with Judith Haywood who went missing several years back."

"Maybe your husband should be informed of this latest information?" Gran prompted.

"Quite right. I'll telephone him straight away."

26

INTERLUDE: LAURIE

Reverend Passwith didn't arrive at Barnstaple Police Station until gone 11.30, an hour later than we'd expected him, although, to be fair to the man, he had telephoned to say he wouldn't be on time as he had a prior appointment. Not that it mattered, for there was a pile of paperwork awaiting us, and very little else. DS Frobisher had taken sick leave, claiming he'd succumbed to whatever the bug circulating through the Force was. I didn't believe a word of it, but the relief of not having him hanging around outweighed any desire to check up on him.

I sat and read all the reports that were, so far, available. Only the skull in the discovered sack of bones had been examined – it was Christmas and time had been limited – but the pathologist's interim statement confirmed his initial opinion that the teeth of the victim were from a forty-to-fifty-year-old female who had died some several years ago, and that he was chasing dental records to confirm an identity. I was convinced, gut feeling if you like, that this was Judith Haywood. He had also confirmed, from two other randomly picked bones, that her corpse had been eaten. I almost threw up at that, but managed to keep my breakfast down, though I suspected I probably looked a bit green round the gills. Even DCI Christopher grimaced a little and swallowed hard as I read that bit of the report aloud. *"Eaten by rodents. Rats probably, although not definitely."*

"So that means she wasn't buried, but left somewhere for them to get at her?" I suggested when my stomach went back to where it should be. "Like in an old shed, or a barn?"

"Risky, wouldn't you think? Easy for someone to find her. Could the remains have been hidden, left in a bin or cupboard? Rats can chew through anything with no trouble."

DCI Christopher had a point, but I contradicted him. "Not if she was dumped somewhere where no one went. The amount of rubbish in some of Haywood's ramshackle outbuildings – no one in their right mind would rummage through them. Or, I wonder if his house has a cellar? Ours does, so does Lower Valley View."

"Perhaps we had better go and rummage there ourselves, then?"

It was not a pleasing prospect, but I had to agree to the proposal.

The interview with Passwith was equally not particularly pleasant, but a few minutes after we'd started, DCI Christopher was called away to the telephone. An urgent call. He came back into the interview room with his usual placid face, although I was getting to know him now after these months of working together. He knew something new.

Passwith was unexpectedly helpful. Yes, as he had already indicated, he had given a lift to Colette Haywood from the station. He'd been there to see his wife off to London. She was ill and was to stay with her younger sister whilst receiving hospital treatment. Which had, sadly, not been successful.

"I see," was all DCI Christopher said, making no visible sign that we'd just eliminated one identity.

"And Colette? What did you do with her?" I asked.

"I dropped her off in the village. Where she went after that, I do not know," came the reply.

"Why did you not go to London with your wife?" DCI Christopher asked. A reasonable question; I could not imagine him sending Mrs Christopher off on her own. Nor would I ever leave Jan to fend for herself in such a situation.

"I had a christening to attend that same week, and a funeral. Besides, she did not want me to accompany her. The sister, you understand, had only a small London flat. There would not have been room for the three of us."

I wondered if there was another reason. If Passwith was as obnoxious to his wife as he was to everyone else, she might have been pleased to have been free of him.

My boss looked through a few papers. "And it's this same sister who now owns and lives in the house in the village?"

I raised an eyebrow. How did he know this? Ah, the telephone call. But who had made it? I relaxed in my chair a little. It didn't take much of a detective's skills to plump for the intrepid Mrs Christopher.

"It is. My wife left her the cottage."

"Does that not gall?" I queried. "Property you lived in going to someone else?"

"Not at all. I always knew the cottage would go to my sister-in-law. I am to rent a nice place here in Barnstaple that will suit me most comfortably. I do not really care for rural life."

The DCI was not going to leave it there, though.

"There's no statement from you in the file to indicate that you gave Miss Haywood a lift that day."

"Is there not? I certainly gave one. At least, I told the Detective Sergeant who was interviewing everyone at the time. Perhaps it has been misfiled?"

I inwardly groaned, from the scanty paperwork we had, I knew the interviewing officer had been Frobisher. A chocolate fireguard had more use than his single cell brain. Which functioned in his nether regions more often than in his head.

"You see, I have a problem," Christopher said, rubbing his chin. "The last person to see Miss Haywood can probably tell us what happened to her."

"I agree," Passwith said somewhat smugly, leaning back in his chair and folding his arms, "but you are implying that she is dead. There is no evidence, beyond her disappearance, to indicate that she is deceased. Unless those remains found in your father's garden, DS Walker, are hers?" When neither of us answered, he continued, "And I would question her father, were I you. He had no love for the girl. Did not treat her, how shall I say? Nicely."

"And why did he not like her?" I asked. "She was his firstborn, after all."

The reverend actually laughed. "Because she was a girl, not a boy, and because he suspected that she was not his child. Now, unless you have further questions, I have things to do today. I assume I may go?"

"I don't think we need detain you much longer, Reverend. Just a couple more things to clear up."

I knew that congenial smile on the DCI's face too well.

"Is there a connection between Colette not being Mr Haywood's daughter, and you stealing the photograph album from Valley View Farm the other day? The photograph in it of Judith's wedding day was significant, perhaps?"

I could tell that the reverend's astonishment was as great as mine.

"I, er... I..." he blustered.

"Are you the father, do you think?" DCI Christopher asked. "Is that why you murdered Judith? Did Colette discover the secret, perhaps, so she also had to be dispatched?"

The reverend's face turned a sort of puce. "An emphatic *no* to both impertinent questions. I take offence at such outrageous suggestions. I am an ordained man of the cloth, I..."

"You are hiding something from us, though, sir, and you did steal that album."

"Chief Inspector, I *borrowed* it, I did not steal it. I did not want anyone in the village realising that I knew Godfrey Haywood and his wife way back when. Especially not Chloë or that gossiping madam in the village shop." Passwith leaned forward across the table. "If, and I stress *if*, I were to ever have an inclination to murder anyone, it would be that woman who keeps the village shop. She is as indiscreet as a giraffe grazing on a cricket pitch."

I didn't point out that giraffes grazed on the leaves of trees, not munched on spirit level-flat lawns, and why would a giraffe be there anyway? But I guess he was speaking figuratively. Although, I could think of several better analogies. Besides, I knew Heather very well and, yes, she was the fount of all village knowledge (gossip), but a kinder, nicer lady you could not wish to meet. Darn good at selling you things you didn't realise you wanted, at what you took to be bargain prices, until you realised her deviousness.

"Tell me about the album?" Christopher asked, his voice neutral.

The reverend shrugged. "The photographer, Joseph Staples and his wife – she is in all the images – passed away a couple of years ago. They were good friends of mine. Ours – myself, Haywood and Judith. Joseph went to God a couple of months ago. He had promised me the album, but he did not tell his son of the promise. Everything went out with the house clearance. I managed to track the album down to the market bookseller, and gave Haywood money to buy it for me. I had an engagement so could not do so myself." He sighed. "But the wretched man spent the money on alcohol. I discovered that your young lady, DS Walker, had purchased the album and my intention had been to acquire it by legal means. Alas, I succumbed to deceitful temptation. For which I profusely apologise." He laid his hands flat on the table. "However, unless you are going to charge me with this minor offence, or something more sinister, I really do need to go. Despite being retired, I still have a small flock to minister to. I am a busy man."

Before the DCI could answer, we were again interrupted. WPC Copper entered and handed me a note. I silently read it, passed it to my boss. (The poor young woman had the most unfortunate name for her occupation; she was endlessly teased with being called things like, 'Constable Copper' and 'Copper Bottom' by fellow workers and criminals alike. Even a magistrate once, had sniggered.)

"*Mmm hmmm,*" the DCI murmured, characteristically as he read the note, then slipped it inside our somewhat sparse information file. "I can't think of any reason, at the moment, to detain you further, Reverend. There may be more questions at a later date, but, for now, you may go."

When the door closed and we were alone, I looked

at the Chief Inspector, pointed to the file. "I suppose we had better follow this new information up?"

He nodded. "I think we should. It isn't every day that forensics come back with a report that hairs found in the skull cavities came from ferrets. Do you happen to know anyone local who keeps ferrets?"

The question was rhetorical.

27

BETTER TAKE A LOOK

Lunch, partaken in the dining room to satisfy Gran, consisted of the expected cold turkey enhanced with delicious home-made apple and damson chutney, although we started with piping hot tomato soup and chunky home-made bread rolls. Aunt Madge makes mouth-watering rolls, which have the secondary advantage of filling a house with the glorious smell of fresh-baked bread. Alf chatted about his greenhouse and making ready to plant his early spring vegetables – hindered by the uncertainty of whether he could use the soil from his compost heap or not. It seemed this subject was one Gran approved of because it involved being thrifty – grow your own rather than buying from these (in her words) 'Obnoxious new, over-priced supermarkets that are pushing the high street greengrocer out of business.'

We'd just finished mopping up the last crumbs when an urgent banging on the front door, loud enough to wake the dead, made us all jump. Banging accompanied by desperate screaming. We all rushed into the hall; Alf flung the door open and Chloë, blood on her hands, face and clothing, fell into his arms. She was in a dreadful state, screaming and crying, taking great gulps of air to accomplish both.

"Dead!" she panted, looking wildly at one then the other of us. "He's dead!"

"Pull yourself together, girl," Gran snapped. "You are not making sense."

Elsie was a little more sensitive. "Come into the kitchen, pet, calm down and explain."

Chloë was having none of it. She pushed Elsie's comforting plaster cast arm aside. "No, no! Is Laurie here? I need the police!"

We looked at each other. Elsie tried again to steer the distraught girl into the kitchen.

"Dad. It's dad! He's killed our old dog and then shot himself!"

"I'll telephone Laurie," Alf said.

———

We waited in the kitchen, with the inevitable cups of tea, for well over an hour. Chloë sipped her tea between gulping intakes of breath and exhaling wild sobs. Elsie had fetched a wet flannel, intending to suggest that the girl clean herself up, but Aunt Madge had shaken her head, whispered, "Best not, in case Toby needs to see any blood patterns."

Almost on cue, Laurie walked in, looking grim.

He shook his head as I started to ask a question, "Any fresh tea on the brew?" was all he said as he sat down next to a still heavily gulping Chloë, who immediately flung her arms round him and burst into new, noisy sobs. Please forgive me – I truly am not being catty – but when *I* cry, my face turns red and blotchy and my eyes look like I'm turning into a panda. Chloë just wailed a lot of loud sobs. Not even her thick mascara ran as mine always did. Though maybe this was because hers was plastered on in multiple layers and had set like cement. I use a Rimmel block and brush. Sparingly. And unlike Chloë, I wash it off each night. (I read in a magazine that Frenchman Eugene Rimmel had a perfumery in Victorian London where he invented the stuff that makes our eyelashes look blacker and better, and in some languages the word *Rimmel* actually *means* mascara! Imagine that!)

Laurie looked at me apologetically as he patted her back. I made a mental note to ask him what he thought about mascara plastered on as thick as mortar.

"We've been at the farm," he said – I'm not sure if he was talking to me, or Chloë, although, probably, all of us. "It's a bit of a... mess." More anguished sobs from Chloë. I noticed that her mascara was beginning to emigrate to Laurie's shirt collar. "Mr Haywood appears to have shot the old sheepdog, and then taken his own life."

He slightly emphasised the word, 'appears'.

"What happened, Chloë? Can you tell me?" he asked gently, easing her away from his shoulder.

Uncle Toby quietly walked in, stood unobtrusively by the back door.

Through hiccups and tearful breaths, Chloë explained that she'd gone out to feed the dog in his kennel and found what she'd found.

"He never did like that dog, never treated him kindly, poor old lad," she spluttered, "said 'e were useless an' nothin' more than another mouth t'feed."

"Did you not hear the shots?" Uncle Toby asked.

Chloë looked startled, unaware that he had been standing there, listening.

"O' course I did, but I thought 'e was out rabbitin' or shootin' crows as 'e always was." Chloë's lip was quivering and more tears trickled from her eyes. Laurie handed her a handkerchief.

"That would have been in the fields or woods, though, wouldn't it? The dog kennel is much nearer to the house," Uncle said, quiet and calm.

"I were in bed," Chloë whispered, "I didn't get up till late. No reason to now as the only stock we got left is the dog." She gulped. "Was the dog. I got dressed, 'ad sommat t'eat in the kitchen. Dad weren't around, but then 'e never is." Gulp. "Was."

"Do you know how to load and shoot a gun, Chloë?" my uncle asked.

"O'course I do? What sort of bloody silly question be that? Anyone on a farm knows 'ow t'shoot on account o' the rats."

"So, you got up and went into the kitchen. Then what?" Laurie prompted.

She looked blankly back at him, as if not comprehending what the question meant. "Then I went out t'feed the dog 'is kitchen scraps."

"Did you touch anything?" Uncle Toby asked. "Did you move the dog? The gun?"

Chloë's lower lip trembled and she again buried her face in Laurie's shoulder. "I, I felt Dad's neck to see if 'e were alive. He were stone cold. Then I moved the gun away, yes," came her muffled response. "I don't know why I did that. I picked it up, dropped it, screamed and ran."

"*Mmm hmm*. You didn't touch the dog?"

"No. Poor old lad was, looked so..."

We were all silent a moment, guessing what she meant.

"Have you anyone you can stay with?" Laurie asked, changing the subject to practical matters.

"Can I stay 'ere with you?"

Elsie frantically shook her head at her son.

"No, Chloë. I'm one of the investigating officers, so that wouldn't be appropriate.

"We'd best go to the station," my uncle announced, "we'll need a written statement, Miss Haywood, and your fingerprints; maybe by the time we've done there, you'll be able to return to your home."

Chloë looked up, startled. "No way! I don't want t'go near the ruddy place, ever again! I've got a friend in King's Nympton. I'll go there."

She sniffed, opened the handbag she was clutching, brought out a handkerchief and blew her nose.

"Just as well I 'ad the foresight to grab this, eh?" she said, bringing out a plastic money purse, putting it back then shutting the bag with a click. "I doubt you'd be kind enough to give *me* five quid, would you, Laurie Walker?"

28

BRING OUT THE BODIES

With all the coming and going up the lane from the SOCO team, pathologist, more police and more than one lurking journalist, we stayed indoors, although what little remained of the Christmas Spirit only materialised in a bottle of gin, with tonic and slices of lemon that we breached once evening started to settle in. Uncle Toby and Laurie came home at around seven-thirty. Dinner was not the jolly occasion of the previous days.

We'd finished clearing the table and doing the washing up, then retired to the sitting room when the telephone rang – Alf answered, but the call was for Uncle Toby; Superintendent Moorcroft wanted a word. Of course, we eavesdropped, although listening didn't help our curiosity that much. All we got was, 'I see', several times, 'If you think so,' and then a few more 'I see's."

"Probably one of the shortest cases I've been on," Uncle Toby announced as he re-joined us. He took a large sip of his after dinner brandy and settled himself into one of the armchairs. "Moorcroft is apparently better now, so he'll be taking over from tomorrow with what's his name, DS Frobisher."

"Good luck to him, then," Laurie muttered.

"He seems to think that the evidence shows that Haywood shot himself, so it's a case of suicide."

"Seems to think?" Gran voiced the query we were all thinking.

"It isn't necessarily easy to kill yourself with a shotgun," Laurie answered for him, one eyebrow raised to signify if he was saying the right thing. "Godfrey Haywood was not a tall man – a good bit shorter than you, Dad – and he didn't have long arms."

"But shotguns are somewhat long?" Alf responded.

"Exactly, Dad."

"And there is the other matter," Uncle Toby added.

Our expressions framed the question: *What other matter?*

"Dental records have revealed that those teeth, and the skull, certainly, were indeed Mrs Haywood. She was shot in the head."

"Poor woman," Elsie murmured.

"Not a nice ending, but at least quick," Gran observed.

"But," Uncle Toby sipped his drink, "now that things have been looked at *properly*, not all the bones were hers."

He got the surprised intake of breath that he had anticipated.

"Who?"

"How?"

"What do you mean?" and such similar verbal astonishments.

"You're going to tell us that some of those bones found in Dad's compost heap belonged to a younger woman, aren't you?" Laurie said.

My Uncle shrugged. "Not quite, but unless Judith

Haywood had two left legs, and three shoulder blades, she had a companion with her."

"Colette?"

"Looks like it."

"They don't suspect me again, do they?" Laurie asked, alarmed.

"No. Superintendent Moorcroft is convinced that Haywood shot them both – at different times, when they walked out on him." He frowned, grimaced. "SOCO have found bone fragments, human fragments, beneath the debris of the ferret compound. A very convenient, and somewhat unpleasant, way of disposing of a corpse or two. Ferrets will eat anything."

I suddenly wished that I hadn't eaten such a big dinner.

Laurie nodded slowly, an hypothesis dawning. "Chloë had unexpectedly sold all her ferrets. If Haywood had buried the bones in their cage, now that the animals were all gone, there was a risk the remaining evidence might be discovered – so he moved everything that was left, in order to shift the blame."

"That is what Moorcroft is surmising. Haywood re-buried the bones in your compost heap, Alf. Not bargaining on his pigs getting out into your garden. The pig's head might have been an additional idea, or even Chloë's little coincidental joke."

We were all quiet a moment, taking in what Uncle Toby had said.

"I suppose we need to question Chloë again, then. About that wire as well, Mum. I'd not be surprised that she rigged it. But how on earth do we tell her that her father seems to have killed her mother and sister?" Laurie said, shaking his head, uncertainly.

"Well, that will be for the Superintendent and DS Frobisher to do, not our problem. That's assuming they ever find her."

Another round of *what* and *how*.

"Chloë was supposed to have gone to King's Nympton – you arranged for her friend to meet her, didn't you?"

"Yes. WPC Copper took her to Barnstaple station, saw her onto the train."

"Her friend was at the station to meet her, but Chloë never got off the train. The friend is rather annoyed at being messed about. Moorcroft has made enquiries. Chloë was seen at Exeter St David's. She bought a single ticket to London, but she could be anywhere between Tiverton and Paddington by now. Or further afield, changing at Bristol Temple Meads."

"But does it matter?" I asked. "Maybe good luck to her for starting a new life somewhere?"

"That could be the case," Gran said, thoughtfully, "but is this Superintendent Moorcroft simply saving on a lot of difficult paperwork and manpower hours? I suspect, DCI Christopher, that you do not think Mr Haywood took his own life, or that he was responsible for the deaths of the two women?"

My uncle raised his glass in an acknowledging salute. "You always were astute, Mrs Brigham. I find it odd that a man should put a gun in his mouth, reach down, with difficulty because he does not have long enough arms, but still manages to pull the trigger. Or that he was able to shoot himself first, and *then* the dog."

Laurie closed his eyes. Rested his head on the back of his chair, suddenly understanding. "When we looked, before the Barnstaple plods arrived, the dog was lying *across* Haywood's arm. And the only fingerprints on the gun were Chloë's?"

"*Mmm hmm*. Although she admitted picking it up, so Moorcroft has discounted her."

"I can understand killing her father," I said quietly,

"but why the dog? And where did she get the money for the train fare?"

"If she was planning on disappearing, who would look after the dog? And she *was* planning, She'd sold the ferrets. Would have got a good few pounds for them."

"I agree," Uncle Toby confirmed, "although whether she also intended to shoot her father, can only be conjecture."

"And her mother and sister?" Elsie asked. "Was that Haywood, do you think?"

Laurie sighed, shook his head. "I think Colette killed their mother. Chloë would have been too young, but I think she knew what had happened. Colette once said to me, after she'd had a few drinks, that she and her sister would rather remember their mother dead than let her abandon them. It never meant anything to me before, but now…"

"So, who shot Colette?" I blurted out.

Laurie took my hand and kissed my palm. "Chloë. For the same reason; anger at being abandoned."

"That's all conjecture, Walker," my uncle admonished gently. "There's no evidence, or proof."

Laurie looked him straight in the eye. "Beg pardon, sir, but there is. Only two people knew I'd given Colette a five-pound note when she, supposedly, left for London. Me and her. Yet, Chloë taunted me about it. If she hadn't seen Colette *after* I'd dropped her at Umberleigh, how did she know?"

"Possibly still conjecture, sergeant. But I happen to think you are correct."

"I think," Alf said after a moment of silence, "we could all do with another drink. It is, after all, sort of, still Christmas."

POSTSCRIPT

Writing these memoirs, recollections – whatever you wish to call them – these many years later after I'd come across my old diaries in the attic during the long days of lockdown in 2020, has resurrected the pleasure of the first Christmas that I spent here in Devon. 1971 had been an eventful year – there were several more to follow, although I did not know it at the time, of course. I enjoyed writing this and revisiting the past, although murder is not exactly an 'enjoyable' subject, but with a DCI as a much-loved uncle, and falling in love with his sergeant, well, crime did become a bit of an everyday topic.

There are a couple of things I must add. Chloë Haywood was never caught or arrested on suspicion of murder because no one was looking for her. Superintendent Moorcroft refused to listen to Uncle Toby's suspicions, and in fact, chastised him for casting doubt on an 'innocent young maid', so the case was closed. Needless to say, my uncle was somewhat 'miffed', as Aunt Madge termed it. Higher Valley View was a council-owned tenant farm; it was sold, pulled down and eight new houses were built on the land.

My children, however, are convinced that I made up everything in this retelling in order to produce a good story. But what is the point of writing a mystery, without a *little* embellishment added in here and there? I assure you, though, most of it happened as I have retold it.

Oh, one more addendum.

On New Year's Day 1972, (*very* early – about 2 a.m) I went up to my bedroom at Valley View, after we'd all been to a wonderful village party, and flopped onto the bed. Bee Bear, resplendent in his new, yellow and black striped jumper, had a velvet pouch tied around his neck by a silk ribbon. I opened the pouch to find a diamond ring and a note inside.

It read: *With all my love, Laurie. Will you marry me*?

Until next time,

Jan

AUTHOR'S NOTE AND
ACKNOWLEDGEMENTS

This is a work of fiction, but for those interested in detail: South Chingford Branch Library, where Jan worked, was a real library. The building (at the time of writing this – 2021) is still there in Hall Lane, but it is no longer a library. I worked there from 1969 when I left Wellington Avenue Secondary School for Girls at the age of sixteen, until 1981. I have many memories – some good, some not so good; such is life when working for the public.

South Molton, Umberleigh, Tiverton, Eggesford, King's Nympton, Chittlehampton and Barnstaple (and Tuly Street) are real locations, but other places mentioned in this story are my invention, including the village where Mr and Mrs Walker lived.

The suspects and tragic murder victims are entirely fictional – all the other characters are also very much made up, apart from shopkeeper Heather, who is a dear friend and is included as I thought she would enjoy having her 'you really *do* need to buy this' skill immortalised in print. Our present-day village community shop is 'manned' and run by volunteers;

back in the 1970s the village had a commercial Post Office-come-general store.

My grateful thanks to various residents (you know who you are!) who took the time and trouble to chat about how things were in the 1970s.

Although I have changed their names, there *was* a station master and his wife and family living at Umberleigh station until the station became 'unmanned' circa 1970 – possibly because of the railway closures made by the government advisor Dr Beeching, although I cannot say this with certainty. I *can* say that the closures are now proving to be a huge mistake, but it is too late to re-open these rural lines. And yes, Umberleigh really *is* a request stop! My thanks to the station master's son for his wonderful memories and information about the years when he lived there with his mother and father. His mother, on whom my character is based as a tribute, *did* keep the station flowerbeds looking perfect, and *did* win several awards. Today, the beds are just as attractive, but maintained by a group of volunteer gardeners – thank you to all of them for their dedication.

My chimney sweep, I discovered when he was at my farmhouse 'sweeping soot' had, as a previous vocation, been a police officer in Barnstaple. Needless to say I pounced on his information, so thank you Mr Sweep, but anything in this story which is incorrect regarding the way Devon and Cornwall Police Force operate is entirely down to my error or imaginative licence, particularly where police procedures are concerned. An outsider DCI temporarily taking over control of a case is one example. I have no idea if this would ever have happened – but this *is* a work of fiction, so in the story-world anything is possible.

As much as I have been able, I have checked and researched the various details mentioned about the early 1970s to ensure they are accurate. I cannot guarantee I have everything right, however. Memory is not always reliable.

I must mention money. A £5 note went a *long* way back in 1971, today the equivalent would be a little over £70, so 25p would now be roughly about £4. My first pay packet in 1969 was just over £100. I thought I was rich!

A quick thank you to Cathy Helms for her patience and expertise for designing the cover and for formatting the text. To Connie Williams, Annie Whitehead, Nicky Galliers and Caz Greenham for their pre-publish scrutiny, and for their ongoing support and enthusiasm. Thank you, ladies!

Finally, I began writing this Jan Christopher Mystery series during the 2020/21 lockdowns of the Covid-19 pandemic as I wanted to write something different to my usual novels. The challenge proved most enjoyable. The view from my study window over 'my' part of the Taw Valley is similar to the view from Jan's guest bedroom. I must stress, however, that I have *never* found any human remains in my compost heap – although we have dug up various cattle bones in the garden, but then, this property used to be a dairy. And our ferrets (Piper and Hamelin) only ate chicken, pigeon, or butcher's scraps obtained from Grattons in Barnstaple.

Oh, and Bee Bear is real.
Well, as real as teddy bears can be.

Helen Hollick
2021

COMING SOON IN 2022

THE JAN CHRISTOPHER MURDER MYSTERIES

Episode 3: *A Mistake Of Murder*

When newly engaged to be married Jan Christopher goes off on her rounds delivering library books to the housebound – she discovers more than she bargained for!

Expected publication: summer 2022

ABOUT THE AUTHOR

Helen Hollick and her family moved from north-east London in January 2013 after finding an eighteenth-century North Devon farm house through being a 'victim' on BBC TV's popular *Escape To The Country* show. The thirteen-acre property was the first one she was shown – and it was love at first sight. She enjoys her new rural life, and has a variety of animals on the farm, including Exmoor ponies and her daughter's string of show jumpers.

First accepted for publication by William Heinemann in 1993 – a week after her fortieth birthday – Helen then became a USA Today Bestseller with her historical novel, *The Forever Queen* (titled *A Hollow Crown in the UK*) with the sequel, *Harold the King* (US: *I Am The Chosen King*) being novels that explore the events that led to the Battle of Hastings in 1066. Her *Pendragon's Banner Trilogy* is a fifth-century version of the Arthurian legend, and she also writes a pirate-based nautical adventure/fantasy series, *The Sea Witch Voyages*. Despite being impaired by the visual disorder of Glaucoma, she is also branching out into the quick read novella, 'Cosy Mystery' genre with the *Jan Christopher Mysteries,* set in the 1970s, with the first in the series, *A Mirror Murder* incorporating her, often hilarious, memories of working for thirteen years as a library assistant.

Her non-fiction books are *Pirates: Truth and Tale*s and *Life of A Smuggler*. She also runs *Discovering Diamonds,* a review blog for historical fiction, a news and events blog for her village and the Community Shop, assists as 'secretary for the day' at her daughter's regular showjumping shows – and occasionally gets time to write...

Website: www.helenhollick.net
Amazon Author Page:
(Universal Link) viewauthor.at/HelenHollick
Newsletter Subscription: tinyletter.com/HelenHollick
Blog: www.ofhistoryandkings.blogspot.com
Facebook: www.facebook.com/HelenHollickAuthor
Twitter: @HelenHollick

ALSO BY HELEN HOLLICK

THE JAN CHRISTOPHER MURDER MYSTERY SERIES

A Mirror Murder

A Mystery Of Murder

To follow:

A Murder By Mistake

(there will be more!)

THE PENDRAGON'S BANNER TRILOGY

The Kingmaking: Book One

Pendragon's Banner: Book Two

Shadow of the King: Book Three

THE SAXON 1066 SERIES

A Hollow Crown (UK edition title)

The Forever Queen (US edition title. USA Today bestseller)

Harold the King (UK edition title)

I Am The Chosen King (US edition title)

1066 Turned Upside Down

(alternative short stories by various authors)

THE SEA WITCH VOYAGES OF
CAPTAIN JESAMIAH ACORNE

Sea Witch: The first voyage

Pirate Code: The second voyage

Bring It Close: The third voyage

Ripples In The Sand: The fourth voyage

On The Account: The fifth voyage

To Follow

Gallows Wake: The sixth voyage

Jamaica Gold: The seventh voyage

When The Mermaid Sings: a short novel prequel.

BETRAYAL

Short stories by various authors

(including a Jesamiah Acorne adventure)

NON-FICTION

Pirates: Truth and Tales

Life Of A Smuggler: In Fact And Fiction

Discovering The Diamond (with Jo Field)

BEFORE YOU GO

HOW TO SAY 'THANK YOU' TO YOUR FAVOURITE
AUTHORS:

Leave a review on Amazon
viewauthor.at/HelenHollick

'Like' and 'follow' where you can

Subscribe to a newsletter

Buy a copy of your favourite book as a present

Spread the word!

Printed in Great Britain
by Amazon